A SAD SONG
SINGING

BOOKS BY THOMAS B. DEWEY

The "Mac" series:

Draw the Curtain Close
Every Bet's a Sure Thing
Prey for Me
The Mean Streets
The Brave, Bad Girls
You've Got Him Cold
The Case of the Chased and the Chaste
How Hard to Kill
A Sad Song Singing
Don't Cry for Long
Portrait of a Dead Heiress
Deadline
Death and Taxes
The King Killers
The Love-Death Thing
The Taurus Trip

The Pete Schoefield Series

And When She Stops
Go To Sleep, Jeannie
Too Hot For Hawaii
The Golden Hooligan
Go, Honeylou
The Girl With The Sweet Plump Knees
The Girl in the Punchbowl
Only on Tuesdays
Nude in Nevada

The Singer Batts Series

Hue and Cry
As Good As Dead
Mourning After
Handle with Fear

Others Novels

My Love Is Violent
Hunter at Large
Can a Mermaid Kill?
A Season of Violence

A SAD SONG SINGING

SINGING

THOMAS B. DEWEY

WILDSIDE PRESS

CHAPTER ONE

The girl came in and sat at the bar, two stools removed from me. She wore a small white cap at an angle on her head and a white suede jacket over a black wool dress, cut low at the top and high at the bottom, and her nylon knees thrust roundly at the bar facing. She had blond hair that hung straight to her shoulders and down her back. Her face was long, narrow, austere, like an advertisement for a French movie. She smoked with dedication, with slow, deep inhalations, and the hand that held the cigarette trembled from time to time, as, possibly, with a little girl trying to be a big girl.

We were in Tony's, across the street from my office. I had been there for an hour; she had just arrived. I'd had a phone call about her from my answering service, a sentimental organization, which had interrupted my nightcap because the girl sounded "so desperate."

"You may tell her," I had said, "where I am and that I will stay until she comes. From there on, it's up to her."

"Thank you," the answering service had said.

"Don't mention it," I had said.

So she had come and sat down and there were only the two of us in the joint, besides Tony, who had heard my end of the phone conversation and stood politely behind the bar now, waiting, while the girl opened her purse and found a cigarette and lit it.

"I'm Mac," I said.

"Yes," she said.

"Would you like something to drink?"

"Well—I—could we talk?"

I shrugged at Tony, who shrugged back and moved away. I tossed off the dregs of my nightcap and swung on my stool toward her.

"Sure," I said. "We'll go over to my office."

"Where is it?"

"Just across the street."

"Oh."

"No hurry," I said. "Finish your cigarette."

She looked at me directly for the first time, with eyes that were dark and frightened.

"All right," she said.

And that's what she did. She sat there and finished her cigarette, methodically, all the way, and snuffed it out when it got down to where it was burning her fingers. Her fingers were slender, like her face, which came to a point at her chin.

I helped her down from the stool. When she stood up, she reached to my shoulder. Her weight had been that of a bundle of dry sticks. I could see now that the clothes she wore were a bad fit, as if they were hand-me-downs, or something she had picked up at a rummage sale.

"My things," she said nervously.

I had seen her stow something in the booth behind us but had forgotten about it. We went over there and the "things" were a battered suitcase and a guitar case.

"Quite a load you're hauling," I said.

"I took a taxi," she said.

That made me feel somewhat better. I reached for both cases, but she slid ahead of me somehow and took the suitcase herself.

"I'll take it," she said.

Its weight seemed to give her no trouble. Carrying the guitar, I opened the door for her, nodded good night to Tony and followed her outside. She hung very close, without touching me except inadvertently now and then with her shoulder. At the street, which was deserted now, though there was still traffic on Michigan Avenue, a block away, she looked in all directions before stepping down from the curb. We crossed over, climbed the front steps and got to my office. When I reached in to snap on a light, she hung back in the hall.

"It's all right," I said. "The blinds are closed."

She came in then, carrying the suitcase, her big eyes taking in the room and a partially exposed section of my living quarters adjoining the office.

"You live here too?" she said.

"Yes. Would you like some coffee?"

"Yes, I would."

I went through the bedroom to the kitchen to get the percolator, and she came along at my heels, watching.

"It's just ordinary coffee," I said, "nothing fancy."

"It's all right."

We went back to the office and I plugged in the pot. She sat on the sofa with the suitcase at her knees and held the handle with both hands, so tightly her knuckles were white.

"You're a musician?" I said, nodding toward the guitar, which was on the sofa beside her.

"No," she said. "I sing a little."

"For a living?"

"Oh no. I'm not good enough."

"Well, you wouldn't be alone in that—"

"And I don't have any songs."

"I see."

"Richie has the songs."

"Richie?"

"Richie Darden—you've heard of him."

"Of course," I lied. "What is your name?"

"Crescentia," she said. "People call me Cress."

"You're Italian?"

"Yes." She put her hand to a strand of her hair. Her long face was intent, serious; her mouth hadn't twitched since I'd set eyes on her. "I dyed my hair," she said.

"For a reason?"

She didn't say anything. She let go of the suitcase, opened her purse and took out a cigarette. I went over and lit it for her, then sat down on the edge of the desk. The percolator started bubbling.

"Why did you come to me?" I asked.

"Because—somebody told me about you—a lawyer I know."

"I mean, for what reason? What is your problem?"

She inhaled deeply on her cigarette.

"You see—it has to do with Richie."

"Richie is your boyfriend? Husband?"

"No, he's my own true love."

"I see."

"This is his—Richie's."

She took hold of the suitcase grip with one hand.

"I'm to take care of it for him, till he gets back. There are people who want it. They'd do anything to get it. They'd kill. They'd kill me to get it."

"Do you know who they are?"

"No."

"Why do they want it?"

"I don't know," she said simply.

"Do you know what's in the suitcase?"

"I—no."

"You haven't opened it?"

"It's locked. Richie has the key."

"Where is Richie now?"

"He's out on the road, singing and collecting songs."

"And he left the suitcase with you."

"Yes."

"Can you get in touch with him?"

"No. See—he's on the road; he doesn't know where he'll be."

"You said he was singing—you mean in coffeehouses and so on? Doesn't he have any advance bookings?"

"No, he just plays where he happens to be, if there's a spot. Besides, even if I could get in touch with him—it's my responsibility. I told Richie I'd take care of it."

"But if somebody's trying to kill you—"

"You don't believe me."

"Yes, I believe you."

She finished her cigarette, totally, as before, and snuffed it out, handling it carefully with her long fingers.

"What is the name of the lawyer who sent you to me?" I asked.

"Lathrop—Willard Lathrop."

I tried to place the name and couldn't.

"Did you tell him what the problem was, about Richie and the suitcase?"

"No," she said. "I just told him I was afraid for my life and he suggested I come to you. I wasn't sure I would make it. They were coming up the front steps of the building when I started out—I got out the back way."

"How many were there?"

"Three."

"You have no idea who they are?"

"No."

I got out a couple of cups and poured coffee. She held the saucer in both hands, almost lovingly, inhaling the aroma.

"I have some money," she said. "I don't expect you to do anything for nothing."

"Well—just what did you have in mind that I might do?"

"I don't know."

"Have you told the police about it?"

She made a face, her first change of expression.

"No," she said. "What good would that do?"

"Might do some good, and it wouldn't cost anything."

"One way or another," she said moodily.

"What would you have done if you hadn't found me?"

"I don't know. I just would have—I don't know."

She savored the coffee gingerly. It occurred to me that she was under-nourished.

"When did you last have something to eat?" I asked. She shrugged.

"I forget."

"Are you hungry?"

"No." She tried the coffee again. "But the coffee is good, thank you."

We drank the coffee. When she finished, meticulously, as with the smoking, draining the last dregs, she set the cup aside. She opened her purse, took out some money and brought it to me, then returned to her seat. There were four tens and three twenties, and I looked at them in my hand, while she looked at me, waiting.

Here's a hundred dollars—think of something.

I finished my coffee, took the money around the desk and dropped it into a drawer.

"Where have you been living?" I asked.

She mentioned an address, north and west.

"Do you have any of your own things in there?" I asked, looking at the suitcase.

"No. I had no time—this was all I could carry."

"We'll have to find a safe place for you, and you'll need some things," I said. "Is your rent paid up?"

"Yes—till tomorrow."

"Do you still have the key?"

"I think so."

She looked through her purse and came up with a key attached to a pasteboard tab.

"Do you want to come with me," I asked, "or would you rather stay here? I think you'd be safe here. I won't be long."

She thought it over behind her big dark eyes. She looked around the room and down at the suitcase and finally she said, "I'll go with you."

"All right, Cress," I said, "let's go then."

I pulled the plug on the coffeepot while she put on her jacket and adjusted the odd little cap. I was holding the door when she got up from the sofa. She took three steps forward, stopped, turned back and picked up the suitcase. When she caught my eye, her thin little figure stiffened and her chin lifted stubbornly.

"All right," I said, "we'll lock it in the trunk."

This we did; she released it to let me stow it in the trunk and stood by while I made sure it was locked. There was no weight to the suitcase.

CHAPTER TWO

After we got across the avenue, it was a fifteen-minute drive to where she lived, in an old section near Division Street. There was still considerable late-night activity on the business streets, but the side streets were empty, and in the solid banks of apartment buildings on both sides few lights burned.

"This is it right here," she said, pointing.

I pulled in a little way beyond the building. Getting out of the car, I examined the neighborhood in all directions. There were no loiterers in sight.

Her building was four stories, walk-up, and there was no entry light. She didn't wait for me to let her out but was standing on the walk, gazing back at the trunk.

"We'd better leave it," I said. "I'll lock the car. We'll be back before anybody can get away with it."

"All right," she said.

I locked both doors and we went up the short front walk, climbed half a dozen steps and went in by the glass front door, which was unlocked. The vestibule had a tile floor and thirty mailboxes set in the wall. The only light was a feeble glow from the inside hall, and I could see that anyone coming home late would have to use a flashlight to get his mail.

We went on through swinging glass doors to the inside hall, which ran straight back to a red-lighted rear exit. Midway along, a narrow staircase reared.

"Mine's on the third floor at the back," she said. I was looking along the hall.

"You said you left by the back door because these three guys were coming in the front."

"Yes."

"But they weren't inside yet?"

"No, they were just opening the outside door. I ran out the back and up the alley to Division Street and there was a taxi."

"How did you know they were after you? Had you seen them before?"

"Yes, they were hanging around The Mill—the coffeehouse—where I work. It's up the street here."

"Had they accosted you at The Mill?"

"Well—yes, sort of. See, I was a waitress there and they were sitting back in a corner—this was the night before last. It's pretty dark in The Mill and these were older fellows and they were just fooling around, I thought. You know, they would make dirty little jokes and—like that—and they kept ordering coffee, and I was about to tell Roger—he's the manager—to get somebody else to wait on them, when one of them said, 'Lay off now,' he said. 'She's Richie Darden's girl.' So they knew who I was."

"Did they ask any questions?"

She looked along the deserted hall, upward to the staircase.

"We'd better get started," I said.

"No," she said, "they didn't ask any questions then. But later, when I was leaving, about two-thirty, they were waiting for me beside the building on the side street.

"'Heard from Richie lately?' one of them asked.

"'I forgot something,' I said, and I went back in The Mill and told Roger there were some fellows outside giving me a bad time and I was afraid to walk home. So Roger said I could wait for him and he would see me home. And about half an hour later we left and he walked me home. We didn't see them around anywhere."

We made the first landing and she was somewhat out of breath, so I eased off on the questions till we reached the third floor. She paused there, leaning against the wall in her borrowed jacket and cap, her long, serious face hovering.

"How did you know they might kill you?" I asked. "That they would kill to get hold of the suitcase?"

Her eyes shifted for a moment, then that pointed chin thrust at me.

"Because," she said, "when I was waiting on them at The Mill, one of them—his jacket pulled open for a second, and he had a gun strapped under his arm—and I saw it."

"I see," I said.

"You still don't believe me."

"Come on," I said, "let's get your things and get back to the car."

"Do you have a gun?" she said.

"Yes, I have one, but I don't like to carry it around."

"Why not?"

"You can get in trouble with a gun."

"Even in self-defense?"

"Even then."

I reached for her hand and she let me lead her down the hall to the rear of the building. Her hand was cold, small and still in mine.

"This one," she said.

I found the key she had given me, unlocked the door and pushed it open.

"Where's the light?" I asked.

"To your left just inside the door."

I reached in and switched on the light.

"All right," I said, "all clear."

We went in and closed the door.

The apartment was small and, though not disorderly, seemed cluttered, because the furniture was too big for the space and there was no discrimination in its placement. This wouldn't be Cress's fault; it was obviously a furnished apartment. An alcove contained a Pullman kitchen, and two pairs of stockings hung over the sink. That was the only disorder in the kitchen; the dishes were put away and the sink and the top of the two-burner gas plate were clean. All this I could see from the main room, in which there were a double bed, neatly made up, a large armchair, and beside the bed, a straight chair with an alarm clock and telephone on its seat. Opposite the foot of the bed was a high chiffonier with a cloth cover on top, a boudoir lamp, a scattering of guitar picks, mingled with bottles of masculine and feminine toiletries, and a large photograph in an easel of a young man in blue jeans and a sport shirt, holding a guitar. The photograph was signed simply, "Richie." He was a muscular fellow, with an Irish smile and thick, black hair. His hands on the guitar were large and strong.

"That's Richie," Cress said.

"Nice-looking fellow," I said.

She was gazing at the picture and I left her with it and turned to a wardrobe set against the wall, between the bathroom door and the door to the hall. It was in two sections, both covered by roll-down doors. I rolled up the left side and there were some jeans and slacks on hangers and two pairs of worn men's shoes.

"Richie was living here too?" I said.

She didn't answer right away and I glanced around. She was looking at me with that little chin in the air.

"Yes," she said proudly, "he was."

"All right," I said.

"Like man and wife," she said firmly.

"Okay, just asking."

I rolled up the other door and saw a pathetically meager array of skirts, sweaters and one cheap print dress. On the floor beneath them, as if to drive the poignancy all the way home, sat a pair of gold evening slippers, in good condition aside from a little dust. They looked as if they had never been worn.

On a shelf above the hangers was a suitcase.

"Could we use this to pack in?" I said.

"Sure," she said.

When I got it down, a flutter of newspapers came with it and drifted to the floor at my feet. I looked on the shelf and saw a large stack of folded papers. I picked up one that had fallen and it was a weekly, published in a small town in Indiana that I had never heard of. I looked at some more of those on the floor and there were a couple from that same town and three or four from other small towns in Indiana and Illinois.

"These papers—" I said.

She looked at them over my shoulder.

"Richie's," she said. "He bought them from a big stand where they sell out-of-town papers."

"Was he looking for notices—about himself?"

"Oh no—he used them for material—for songs. Richie said small-town newspapers were one of the best places to get ideas for where to look for songs. 'That's where folks really live,' he used to say."

"I see," I said.

I opened the suitcase on the bed and she began to gather up the things off the chiffonier. I went to the wardrobe again and started through Richie's pockets, surreptitiously, watching her with an edge of my vision. She didn't seem to notice. She lingered awhile over the photograph, finally folded it into one of her sweaters and laid it away in the suitcase. I didn't find anything in the jeans and I had my hand in one of the pockets of some slacks when she said:

"What are you looking for?"

It startled me and I had no ready answer.

"Just nosy," I said. "That's my business."

"You won't find anything in his clothes. I checked all his pockets before I took them to the laundry."

"Oh," I said.

"You're a hard man to convince."

"Yeah," I said. "Well, Cress, that's my business, too, being hard to convince. How long has Richie been gone?"

"About a month."

"And you haven't heard anything from him?"

"No, but I didn't expect to. When would he write letters? Most of the time he's probably way back in the country somewhere and there's no post office even."

"Uh-huh," I said.

I opened a drawer in the chiffonier and there was a collection of hand-outs and fliers in various sizes and colors, some of them with Richie's picture and an announcement of an appearance somewhere. There were half a dozen brochures from The Mill, featuring Richie along with a group called the Nelsons, three boys and three guitars.

I picked out three or four of them with Richie's picture on them and folded them into my pocket. I couldn't tell whether she noticed or not. She had cleared out her side of the wardrobe and was taking down the jeans and slacks. I was still pawing through the papers in the chiffonier and my hand ran across a sharp edge, not quite hard enough to draw blood, but causing me to jerk away from it. Cress looked at me.

"Have you given notice here yet?" I asked.

"No—is it important?"

"I guess not, as long as the rent's paid. How about your job?"

"I told Roger I wouldn't be at work for a while."

"Did you tell him why?"

"No, but maybe he guessed. He's not stupid."

Feeling around carefully, I had found the handle of a long knife. I brushed the papers away from it and saw it was a stiletto type, razor sharp on the edges and pointed like a needle; a knife to kill with.

"This was Richie's?" I said, holding it up.

She shook her head vaguely.

"I guess so. I never saw it before."

I wrapped it in my handkerchief to dull the edges and laid it in the suit-case on top of a pair of his slacks. Cress went to the chiffonier and started taking out some men's shirts and a small wad of feminine undergarments. I looked into the bathroom, and it was clean and contained nothing except the usual facilities. When I got back, Cress was wrapping Richie's shoes in some of the newspapers and laying them in on top of the other things in the case, which was well filled without being stuffed.

"I guess that's everything," she said.

"There were some stockings in the kitchen."

"Oh, yes, I forgot."

She went out there and I looked through the rest of the chiffonier with-out finding anything. I stood beside her, leaning over the bed, while she put the stockings in the suitcase.

"Shall we close it now?" I asked.

"I guess so. I can't think of anything else."

I pulled the lid up and over and let it fall. It didn't quite click shut. I was leaning over it, preparing to push it down, when she spoke sharply under her breath:

"Listen…!"

She had good ears. By the time I heard them, the steps were at the door, the hand on the knob. Every hair on my body stood straight up. I pushed at her with my right hand and moved along the bed to the straight chair. Cress made it to the other side of the bed. I picked up the telephone and tossed it onto the bed.

"Call the police," I said.

The door opened and they came in. I had time to half turn, and two of them were into the room and I could see the third one behind them.

Nobody said anything. It wasn't that kind of a party. I flipped the lid of the suitcase back and groped for the knife, now buried under shoes and stockings. I couldn't find it. One of the trio started around the bed and another one approached me. I could hear Cress dialing the telephone. The bed lurched heavily as the nearest of the three came at me. There was a tearing sound and I knew somebody had ripped the phone from the wall connection. Cress gasped. I brought one of the shoes up out of the suitcase and rapped the heel into the guy's nose. By then I had found my balance and I twisted and hit him in the belly. It stopped him all right, but the third one was coming around him and he had a gun in his hand, holding it by the muzzle. He lifted it and I ducked into him in the midsection. The gun butt came down hard on my kidneys, but he was off balance. I kept after him, to get into the clear, and when he was ready to hit me again I kicked at him where it would hurt bad and shouldered him into the chiffonier. I heard him grunt and his feet slip under him.

The first one jumped on my back then and we were in it good. Nothing scientific—just desperate clawing and slugging—them or us, right now. I twisted out from under the one and hit the other with all I had, as low under the ribs as I could get any drive into. It stopped his heart for a second and he sagged down, clawing the cover off the chiffonier as he came. I turned into the other one, who somehow had come by the gun, or had one of his own, and the only chance I had was to get inside and grapple with him. He hit me once on the cheekbone and a glancing blow on the side of the head and I couldn't see well. I kept hitting him with both hands, and he backed off and swung at me again but lost his footing and fell against the wall beside the door. I was gasping for breath, trying to clear my head and wondering what was happening to Cress and why somebody didn't come around to see what the noise was about. But they never come. They stay home and pound on the ceiling—or call the manager.

So call! I thought frantically.

The one on the floor had turned the gun around to make full use of it and I brought my left foot down on his wrist on the floor and kicked at his face with my right. I connected well enough to quiet him, but it threw me backward onto the bed. The third guy was trying to drag the suitcase across the bed while, as it turned out, holding Cress by the neck with his free arm, with his hand clamped over her mouth. I rolled up over the suitcase and grabbed him by the lapels of his jacket. He let go of the suitcase and hit at me, but he had too many irons in the fire. I pulled myself up by his jacket and pushed, and when he reared back, I hit him in the stomach. He doubled down on his knees and I looked around in time to see the one with the gun coming across the bed at me.

"All right—" he said.

But things were going for me now and I couldn't have stopped if I'd wanted to. I dived into him at his knees and the luck held; he lost his balance on the shifting springs and fell backward and I heard the gun bang against the wall and drop. I swam on over the edge of the bed and got my hands on it, and when he picked himself up, I was holding it by the butt and he saw that and stopped.

We were both shaking like leaves in the wind. I didn't dare stick my finger inside the trigger guard for fear of squeezing off unintentionally. I don't know whether he noticed that or not, but he kept staring at my hand and he didn't come on. He was smallish, with black-rimmed eyes, scrawny in the throat. He looked young, twenty, twenty-one maybe. There was a cut on his left cheek where I had hit him at some time. The other two I could see only vaguely in the background, not to identify. There was a lot of sweat or something running into my eyes and my throat kept clogging.

"Back off," I managed to say.

He hung there for a few seconds, staring at me with his mouth open, then backed away toward the door.

"Hold it," I said.

He stopped and I fought for breath and time. They were all over the room and I couldn't figure out how to gather them up. They could have taken me then, the way they were spread out, and I don't know why they didn't, except that I would have hit at least one of them and none of them knew but that it might be him.

The standoff lasted about three seconds. Then there were scrambling, lurching movements on the bed, over my left shoulder. I looked around and Cress was on her knees with her right hand in the suitcase and the one I had brought down by the bed was going after her. I heard a strangled protest from the one at the door and when I got my eyes on him, he had the door open and was going out. I couldn't shoot him going away, for various good and bad reasons.

The third one had got up and was hanging onto the chiffonier, still gasping for breath. I was on my knees. Pushing up to my feet, I turned to the bed. Cress had the long knife in her hand, trying to jab at the other guy, who was holding her off with both hands. I yelled at him and he looked into the gun dead level and growled something. There were heavy steps and I knew the one by the chiffonier had left us. I could hear him going down the hall. Somewhere in the building a voice swore loudly.

On the bed, he was holding Cress down by her wrists, crouching over her. I wiggled the gun at him.

"Get up off her, no fooling," I said.

He was cut in two or three places on the face and neck, but superficially. He had a long nose, slightly bent to one side, and black hair cut square and low across his forehead, with deep sideburns. He stared at the gun for about a watch tick and a half, then let go of Cress's wrists and started back off the bed.

At least I'll hang onto this one, I was thinking.

Then Cress, in fury and frustration, lunged up at him with the knife. It brought her between us and the gun was useless. The guy threw himself to one side, away from her, rolled off the end of the bed and kept going, on his knees at first, then, with a lunge, on his feet. I ran along the bed to head him off and tripped over the disarranged bedclothes. I went down helplessly, sprawling, and banged my head against the wall near the door. It stunned me and I went through a period of buzzing in the head and then some silence.

* * * *

When I came to, my first impression was of pain in my right hand. Working the fingers around, I found they had a death grip on the gun, which was bruising my knuckles against the wall.

Anyway, I thought, I held onto the gun.

Then I felt nausea and next a warm wetness on the upturned side of my face. I could hear Cress's voice nearby but couldn't make out the words. Finally I understood her to say:

"…you all right?"

I rolled onto my back and she was on her knees on the floor with this wet cloth in her hand. My head was still clanging and I felt lethargic. She asked again:

"Are you all right?"

"Yeah, I'm all right," I said. "How about you?"

"I'm all right. They didn't hurt me."

"I'm glad."

She put the cloth on my forehead and pressed lightly, then removed it.

"Do you believe me now?" she said.

"I believe you," I said.

My left eye was swollen and sightless. I must have looked pretty funny, lying there peering up at her. Anyway, she smiled, not much, but enough to draw up the corners of her mouth and soften the hard line of that stubborn chin. It was the first smile out of her. When she saw I had noticed, she put the cloth over my eyes. I left it for a minute, then took it off and laid it in her hand.

"We'd better pick up the stuff and go," I said.

It took me some time to get up, but once on my feet, I could move all right. All the pain was in my knees and head and I knew it would go away.

Cress's hair was mussed; she had lost the little white cap and there was a bruise on her cheekbone, but she was functional. I watched her walk away to the bathroom, with the cloth in her long fingers, and she walked straight and firm.

Richie Darden, I thought, you got a good woman there. I wonder where you think you are.

When she came back, I was repacking the suitcase on the bed.

"Hey, Cress," I said, "how old are you?"

"Why?" she said.

"Just wondered."

After a minute she said, "Seventeen."

I closed the suitcase, picked up the gun, and we turned off the light and got out of there. I carried the gun in my hand, out in the open. It felt kind of silly, but then, it didn't feel too bad either.

CHAPTER THREE

Cress was stretched out under a blanket on the couch in the office, and I was preparing to clean up, when I discovered I'd lost my wallet. It contained little cash but several credit cards, my driver's license and a photostat of my professional license, everything necessary to lead the finder straight home. If the three musclemen had not gone back to the apartment after we left, they were not really thorough. Even if they hadn't gone back, they surely would have lingered long enough to spot my car and license number, and soon enough they would know me and my address.

I thought about it while washing up and smoothing out the lumps on my head and face. When I finished, I was in no shape to pose for any Vitalis ads, but I wasn't too hideous. I could see all right with the one eye and there was only one spot where a small strip of adhesive tape was essential. The pain had dulled to a headache and my knees had settled down. The bad thing I had left was nerves. Somebody came into the building and before the sound of the outer door had faded, I was in the office with the gun in my hand. Then footsteps clomped through the hall and started upstairs and I knew it was another tenant. There was no sound from the couch, and when I took a close look at Cress, she was asleep.

I got into a fresh shirt and a tie, took some money and the original of my license from the strongbox on the closet shelf, and sat down at the desk in the dark. After a while I got up and looked out through the blinds. Tony's joint was closed and I couldn't see anything hanging around on the street. It didn't help much. I'd have felt better if I'd seen something, anything. The next time they would come prepared.

For myself alone the problem was simple; I could lock the doors, stick the gun under my pillow and catch some sleep. But the trouble had more than doubled, and the square root of it was a slender, seventeen-year-old girl with long, blond hair.

I went back to the bedroom, got down a suitcase of my own and put some things in it. The way it was going, I thought, we'd have enough luggage for a world tour. It was all stacked in the middle of the office: the guitar and her suitcase and the one Richie had left with her, which she had insisted on bringing in from the car. I put mine down with the rest of it and sat on the edge of the couch.

She was sleeping on her back, her face half hidden in her hair. She didn't wake when I sat down, but her face twisted, frowning, then relaxed slowly. I looked at my watch and it was getting on to three o'clock. All the hours between now and daylight would be bad ones. She was young; if she could go to sleep so easily, she could wake up.

I put the back of my hand to her cheek and joggled her lightly. She stretched, lifting her arms. Her eyes blinked and closed.

"Cress," I said quietly. "Hey, Cress—come on."

Her arms rose again and went around my neck. Stretching upward, she opened her eyes and mouth, searching. I shook her a little and she woke up. She clung to my neck for a while, blinking me into focus, then let her arms fall away.

"Oh," she said, yawning, "I thought it was Richie."

"I'm sorry," I said. "I guess I'll have to do for now. Can you wake up? It's time to go."

"Go where?"

"I don't know exactly. Somewhere else."

She looked thoughtful.

"Yes," she said, "I guess so."

So she knew why, and I didn't bother to explain about losing the wallet.

"If you want to freshen up," I said, "I'll load the things in the car."

"All right."

I found a clean towel for her and left her alone. I took the guitar and my own suitcase and carried them out to the car. It was a raw night, with a stiff breeze off the lake at my back. I locked the trunk and took a good long look around the neighborhood. There was nothing more than I had seen from the window, so I felt about the same as before, only colder.

Inside, she was still in the bathroom. I picked up the other two suitcases and took them to the car. The trunk was well loaded now, but I managed to get everything in and lock it. When I got back this time, she was coming from the bedroom, smelling of soap. Her white jacket was on the sofa and I helped her into it.

"Looks as if you lost your hat," I said.

"Yeah," she said.

"Excuse me," I said, and went into the bedroom.

I took off my jacket, got my gun from the closet and put it on, with the damn harness and all, and my jacket over it. When I rejoined her in the office, she had picked up the gun I had saved from the fracas and was turning it in her hand, examining it. It was a .38 revolver and far too big for her.

"You want this one, too?" she asked.

"Not exactly," I said, "but I don't want to leave it lying around—for children to play with."

She replaced it on the desk with something of a bang. I opened a desk drawer, took out the money she had given me and put it in her hand.

"There are only two things certain in life," I said. "Just in case we should get separated, you'll need some money."

She looked at me curiously, then at the money in her fist.

"You're funny," she said.

"Well, I guess it's not one of my serious days."

She pushed the money into a pocket of the suede jacket and I put the .38 into a pocket of my own.

"Shall we blow?" I said.

She came along without hesitation. At the top of the steps I cased the street in both directions, then led her to the car, briskly but not at a run. She hadn't shown any signs of panic and I didn't want any to develop. I decided she had been scared at first for fear I would laugh at her story, and what would she do then? Now that was over with and she didn't seem scared any more.

* * * *

I drove around the Near North Side for a few minutes, got on Lake Shore Drive and went out north, then came off it, heading for the Loop on Michigan Avenue. By then I was satisfied we weren't being chased.

Cress didn't show any curiosity. Maybe she had figured it out for herself, or maybe she just didn't give a damn. As it turned out, I discovered, when I pulled into the garage of a medium-sized commercial hotel downtown, she was asleep.

I had picked the place because I knew it to be well run and to have a good house cop; because everything she would need was inside, so she wouldn't have to go out on the street; and because it was a handy location for the work I would have to do the next day—or later that same day, come to think of it.

We had two rooms, adjoining, with the connecting door unlocked. While she sat at the dressing table, brushing her long hair, I explained that I would go out in the morning and wasn't sure when I'd get back but that she would be all right here. If she needed anything, all she had to do was to get on the phone and tell the desk what she wanted and somebody would bring it up. She could order her meals from room service. She wouldn't have to leave the hotel.

"I feel like a queen on a white horse," she said.

"All right. That's good," I said.

"That's the way Richie always made me feel," she said.

"Was it at The Mill you first met Richie Darden?"

"Yes—at The Mill—I was working there and he came—he wasn't on the show, but he had his guitar and naturally somebody noticed and they all began clapping and calling for him. I was waiting on him and when they started this, Richie asked me, 'Do you think I should?' And I said, 'Sure—can you sing?' 'I know a few songs,' he said. So I said, 'Go ahead then,' and Richie said, 'Okay, honey, but you pay attention, because I'll be singing them all to you.' Which he did—right to me, and when he finished, I was crying."

She was crying a little now, and the brushing had stopped. Her mouth moved and after a while I realized she was singing, softly, on her breath, to her own reflection in the mirror, with that long hair down on her shoulders. It was a familiar song, simple and plaintive; I had heard it before somewhere, or maybe I just thought I had. Her voice was small and not always strictly true; it lacked color and confidence, but she sang straight from the heart.

> *The joys of love*
> *Are but a moment long;*
> *The pain of love endures*
> *The whole life long.*
>
> *My love loves me,*
> *And all the wonders I see—*
> *A rainbow shines in my window,*
> *My love loves me.*
>
> *And now he's gone*
> *Like a dream that fades into dawn;*
> *But the words stay, locked in my heartstrings,*
> *My love loves me.*

She faltered at the end and she was crying in earnest now, big tears welling from her eyes and flowing down that narrow, sad face. She put her head down on her arms.

"Richie…!" she cried. "Richie—come back."

I had no words of comfort for her. There was too much time between us. What hurts like death at seventeen may be a muffled pang at my age, and there is no way to explain this across the years.

I looked at Richie Darden's suitcase, next to hers, and at the guitar and wondered what that world was like inside their heads.

"Richie—" she moaned into her arms.

I put my hand on her shoulder, but she took no notice.

"Try to get a little sleep," I said. "I'll be right in the next room."

I left her alone, closing the door between us to give her privacy. I undressed, put on pajamas and a dressing gown, in case I should have to get up in a hurry, and got into bed. With nothing to distract it, my headache got in some concentrated licks, but gradually I learned to relax under it, and in time it dulled. I checked two or three times and the light still showed under the connecting door. I dozed off and the next time I checked, the light was out. I settled back, ready to sleep, and the door opened. I lifted my head and after a minute I could see her standing in the dark, wearing a night gown and some sort of bathrobe that was too long for her and fell in folds on the floor around her feet.

"Mac—" she said.

"Yes, Cress?"

"Can we leave the door open?"

"Sure. Any way you want it."

She lingered in the doorway. Her hand came up and brushed her hair back from her face.

"Are you frightened, Cress?" I asked.

I got up on my elbow. She lifted the robe clear of the floor and came to the bed, sat on the edge of it with her hands in her lap.

"No—not exactly," she said. "I was just thinking—what are you going to do tomorrow?"

"I'm going to visit the mug shop—rogues' gallery—and see if I can get a make on those three guys we had the spat with. And then I thought I would talk to your friend Roger at The Mill and see what he knows."

"Well, when Richie comes back," she said, "and I'm not there anymore, in that apartment—how will he find me?"

"Easy. I'll make a connection with Roger and we'll keep in touch with him."

"Oh."

Pretty soon she said, "When I'm here alone all day, will it be all right if I play my guitar a little?"

"Sure."

"Because I can get pretty lonely, just sitting around. But if I can play the guitar—"

"You can absolutely play the guitar as much as you want to."

"All right," she said.

She got up, holding the long robe off the floor, and started away. Then she came back, leaned over the bed and kissed me on the mouth, quickly, without warning.

"Thanks, Mac," she said. "I'm sorry I cried."

"Don't be worrying about that," I said. "Crying's good for you, as long as you can stop when you have to."

"Good night, Mac…"

She started off, then returned once more.

"Listen—you said something about—only two things are certain in life. What are they?"

"Oh—that's an old cliché."

"But what are the two things?"

"Death and taxes."

"Death and taxes," she said thoughtfully. "Death and taxes—I like that."

"You're among the few," I said.

"Okay—'night, now," she said.

She waved her hand and ran into her own room, leaving the door open. I had the distinct impression that she went to bed happy because of death and taxes.

CHAPTER FOUR

My call came at ten o'clock and I replied gruffly, then remembered I had asked for it. I felt as if I were made out of burned-out wire, but I managed to make the shower and after about fifteen minutes I woke up enough to get dressed. Cress was asleep, and I left a note for her and went out in silence. Before leaving the hotel, I looked up the house detective, whom I knew, and asked him to keep an eye on the room. He asked no questions and I knew I could depend on him.

At the place where they keep the pictures of the misguided, I had to make my report to an officer who was unknown to me. He was young and efficient and not too interested, especially when he found out who I was.

"Private eye, huh?" he said. "Were you some place you shouldn't have been?"

"I was some place I was hired to be," I said.

He grunted and made a note.

"Will you sign a complaint?" he asked with suspicion.

"What good would it do to sign a complaint against persons unknown?" I said. "If I could see some pictures…"

He thought it over and gave me a slip of paper that got me through a couple of doors, and after a while I was looking at pictures. There were a hell of a lot of them and the prospect was gloomy. I could remember clearly only the youngish one with the black-rimmed eyes. The one with the distorted nose I had seen through a red film and the rest of his features were a montage in my memory. The third was a total blank.

An Identification officer was with me at first and he got called away. He was replaced by a detective sergeant whom I knew from my old days on the force. By the time the first man left, I had studied so many pictures the faces were beginning to blend into a composite monstrosity, and I took a few turns around the room to get my blood going and to rest my eyes— or eye; the one was still swollen more or less shut. The third time around, without thinking much about it, I took out one of the fliers with Richie Darden's picture on it and looked at it for a change. It was somebody I knew, in a way, and it gave me a sort of orientation. I was looking at it when Sergeant Schnell came in, and I dropped it on the table along with the mug shots.

"Well, well," he said, "looky there. If it ain't the old bird dog—run into some kind of a door."

"Hello, Kegs," I said.

Schnell was German, with a taste for beer, and was always in trouble with the physical-fitness outfit.

"You run into it kind of hard, huh?" he said.

"Kind of. What's new?"

He eased himself into a creaking armchair and his belly came to uneasy rest against the edge of the table.

"You know how it goes," he said. "I ain't had too much sleep lately for sure. Who you lookin' for here?"

"Three guys," I said.

"Why?"

"A fellow left a suitcase with his girlfriend. These three seem to want it. Last night they came to get it and I happened to be there."

"Where was this? What neighborhood?"

I told him and he nodded sagely—whatever that meant. Pretty soon he said:

"You mean all three of 'em got away?"

"Yeah."

"And you had the gun?"

"Yeah."

"Where's the gun?"

"I left it home."

"You should turn that in."

"I forgot it. I'll bring it around later."

"Did you get a number off it?"

"There was no number on it that was legible."

"Great."

He looked depressed.

"These rascals say anything, like names or anything?"

"Nothing," I said. "The one I remember best was a young guy with black rings around his eyes."

"What's in the suitcase that they want so bad?"

"I don't know."

"You don't know?"

"That's right."

"Does the girlfriend know?"

"She says not."

"Can't you open it, for God's sake?"

"Not without permission."

He snorted and ran his hands through his hair.

"Where's the boyfriend now?"

"She doesn't know."

"What's his name?"

"I'd rather not say."

"Is it a heavy suitcase, like full of printing plates or something?"

"No, it's very light."

"Uh-huh." He thought about that. "Heroin don't weigh much."

I had thought of that myself but had passed over it, maybe because I wanted to. I shrugged.

"A suitcase full—" I said.

"But nobody would have a suitcase full. Nobody could afford it."

"Yeah," I said.

So we were back at the starting line.

"Well, you found any suspects here in the likenesses?"

"Not yet."

"Let's get lookin'."

We started turning pages. Every once in a while a face would strike some chord in Schnell's memory and he'd chuckle or grunt or swear. He told me a story about one of them—a counterfeiter named "Good Sam," who had scruples about passing his product among innocent, unsuspecting people. He would only dump it on other hoodlums, gamblers and con men and such, and he finally turned himself in for his own protection.

We had gone far beyond Good Sam, had been at it for three quarters of an hour, before I found the one I was looking for, the young guy with the rings around his eyes. The picture was clear and recent and it was him all right.

"Let's see," Schnell said, "he's nobody to me—'Carryl Borchard—age, twenty-two, five, ten and a half, one forty-five pounds, black hair, dark eyes, tending to be shadowed.' What else? 'Probation, stolen car, at eighteen; parole from armed robbery—a very light rap...' Not much of a record. 'Last known address...' It don't say. Great."

"Can you find out?"

"Somewhere."

There was a phone on the wall and Schnell went to it and put in a call. After a while he came back and sat down beside me.

"You want us to bring him in?"

"Not yet."

"You don't plan to file no complaint?"

"Maybe."

I saw the Richie Darden flier lying on the table, picked it up and started to put it in my pocket. Schnell reached for it and took it out of my hand.

"Who you got there?" he said. Then, "Oh—one of them."

"What do you mean, 'one of them'?" I said.

"You know what I mean—troublemakers. If it wasn't for the Civil Liberties Union, we'd run 'em all out of town."

"I've heard that before."

But Schnell was serious.

"They're Commies, for Christ's sake!" he said. "Freedom Riders"— he snorted—"and that peace march!"

"It's a free country."

"Listen, when you and I was that age, we wouldn't of gone for a peace march—more like the other way around."

"Yeah," I said. "When you and I were that age, we wanted a war to see what it was like with those French girls our pappies told us about. We didn't figure on Guadalcanal—or the Aleutian Islands."

Schnell regarded me through half-closed eyes.

"You're talkin' pretty snotty," he said, "for a man with a renewable license."

"I guess I'm sore for getting pushed around. Excuse me."

The phone tingled and I put the Richie Darden thing in my pocket and reset my hat on my head. Schnell was on the phone for about a minute.

"Carryl Borchard," he said, "last known address."

He dropped a piece of notebook paper on the table and I picked it up. The address was far out on the West Side and I looked at my watch.

"Don't let me keep you," Schnell said.

"Thanks for everything," I said. "I'll check in with you."

"Please," he said.

* * * *

Carryl Borchard's address was a housing development about ten years old. It contained maybe two thousand units, spread over a couple of acres of cleared ground. When new, it had been an improvement over the old tenements, but ten years and a generation of vandals can do a lot of damage. The outside walls and the entry halls had been stripped of every removable fixture. The lawn was no longer maintained, and a pathetic jumble of playground equipment angled starkly from a desert landscape of sand and brown weeds. Inside, climbing to the second floor and Borchard's apartment, I saw that the walls had been defaced in every imaginable way and the odor was predominantly of garbage. I had seen old LaSalle Street flea bags with a more appealing décor—and aroma.

I knocked on Borchard's door—with my knuckles, there being only three holes in the panel now where the original metal knocker had been—and waited quite a long time. I had my hand up to give it another rap when the door was opened from inside.

The young woman who had opened it held a very small baby in one arm. She was well advanced in pregnancy, and a little girl of about two looked around and up at me from behind her mother's skirt. The woman brushed at a lock of hair that had fallen across her face and the baby began to cry.

"I'd like to talk to Carryl Borchard," I said.

She looked at me with eyes that seemed to have moved backward into her head, as if afraid to come out and look around.

"What do you want with him?" she said.

"Just talk."

"You from the police?"

"No, ma'am."

She looked at me some more, disbelieving.

"Just a minute," she said, and closed the door.

I waited three minutes and the door opened again and it was him.

"Yeah?" he said.

He looked at me without recognition. Inside, the baby was crying lustily now. There was the sound of a slap and the little girl began to howl. Borchard came into the hall, closing the door behind him. At about the same moment the door clicked shut, he remembered me and where he had seen me before. He went stiff; his hands moved out from his body a few inches, and he slid along the wall away from the door and set his shoulders against it.

"What do you want?" he said.

"I want some information."

"I don't know anything about it. It was the other two—I just went along—"

"Well, you were there and I can't find the others. Who are they?"

He moved his head from side to side against the wall.

"Think about it," I said, "while I go into some other matters. What about Richie Darden?"

"What do you mean—what about him?"

"What do you want with him or his girl?"

"Nothing I know of—"

"Come on. What's in the suitcase?"

"I don't know. Honest, I don't know. Nobody told me nothing."

I stood there and he looked at me for a while and then he looked at something else. He had a nervous thing with the corner of his mouth.

"Listen," I said, "I went down to the place and looked you up. It's up to me whether I sign a complaint, so they can take you in. You have a little record, enough, I think. You can go down and talk to them, the hard way, or you can talk to me now."

"I don't even know who you are—"

"I'm a private detective. I've got a license if you want to see it."

"All right, what do you want?"

"Who are the other two guys? Names and addresses, please."

"I don't know—"

"Just a couple of strangers you ran into, huh? Said come on, let's go up here and get a suitcase."

"They never told me—"

"Where did you meet them?"

"In some joint—"

"What joint?"

"I mean, one of them coffeehouses—"

"The Mill?"

"No, another one, on the South Side."

"What's the name of it?"

"I don't even know."

"What have you got to do with coffeehouses?"

"Nothing—they was looking for this Richie Darden."

"You know Richie Darden?"

"No, I don't know him—"

"But they wanted you to lead them to him."

"No—I just said I read about him being at The Mill—"

"How did you know he had a girlfriend and who she was?"

"I didn't—just hung around there and found out—"

"Why did they want to see Richie Darden?"

"I don't know."

"What's in the suitcase?"

"I don't know."

I looked at him and he wasn't looking at me anymore at all.

"You'd rather go through the whole routine, huh?" I said. "Let them pick you up and line you up and maybe shove you around some—"

"I tell you the God's truth, I don't know! They're from out of town—somewhere—I don't know."

There was a rush of small feet inside the apartment; the door flew open and the little girl ran out, found Borchard and ran to him, wrapping her arms around his legs, sobbing. He looked down at her without touching her. Then he looked at me.

"All right, Borchard," I said, "for now."

I went off down the hall, not wasting any time because I was on the verge of getting sick to my stomach.

My car was on the street, directly opposite the project, and I got in it and sat there, waiting. I didn't have to wait long. Borchard came out of the building, in his shirt sleeves, walked to the main sidewalk and down the street half a block to a public phone booth. He went in and made a call and he was there about three or four minutes, then he came back, went into the building, and I waited a while longer, but he didn't reappear.

I drove back toward town, found a place to eat and had a quick lunch. It was after two o'clock and the service was very good, but the food was terrible. I left what I couldn't choke down, drove over to Division Street and parked in front of The Mill.

The entrance was a narrow opening in a façade painted to resemble a barn door, but inside it was spacious and well lighted. There was a large room off to my right with a display of phonograph records and some books and magazines. Eight or ten kids in jeans and sweat shirts and similar apparel were in the room, sitting around or browsing through records. Two of them had guitars. There were both male and female and I could tell them apart, usually, by the length of their hair and, of course, in profile.

A front hall led past the record display to a curtained doorway that evidently led to the entertainment area. Near the door was a ticket booth. A flight of stairs rose from the hall to a gallery that would overlook the theater. There was nobody in the ticket booth, and as I looked around, a girl came down the stairs. She was wearing slacks and a sweater and big horn-rimmed glasses.

"Looking for Roger…" I said.

She waved up the stairs.

"He's up there," she said, "working on the lights."

She went on toward the record room and disappeared. I climbed eight or ten steps into a gallery, where a guy about thirty was on his hands and knees with a screwdriver and the disassembled parts of a baby spotlight around him. I waited till he looked up.

"I'm a friend of Cress's, Richie Darden's girl," I said.

"Hi," he said pleasantly. "Know anything about electricity?"

"Very little."

"Me, too. What was it about Cress? Is she all right?"

"She's in a safe place," I said.

Downstairs somebody started strumming a guitar, low and sad and faraway. The gallery was open along the back and there was a bank of lights aimed at the stage below. The stage was a small platform about a foot higher than the floor, which was covered with chairs and small tables. I estimated the capacity of the house to be about two hundred.

"There!" the guy said, and laid down the screwdriver. "I got it apart, maybe before night I can get it back together."

He got on his feet, dusted his hands on his trousers and held one of them out to me.

"Roger Semple," he said. "What can I do for you?"

"I hoped I could get a line on Richie Darden," I said.

He found a cigarette and lit it and took a couple of drags on it.

"Excuse me for asking," he said, "but what's the connection? I mean, you said you're a friend of Cress's—"

I got out my license and he peered at it.

"She came to me for help," I said, "about those three goons—"

"Oh, them," he said. "I remember. She was scared—I walked her home the other night."

He didn't seem to take it very seriously.

"Have they been back?" I asked him.

"No," he said, "haven't seen them. I didn't even see them the other night. It was only that Cress told me about it and was obviously bugged, so I couldn't let her go home alone—"

"She had good reason, as it turned out," I said, "but that's history now."

"Oh?" he said. "I didn't mean to put it down. Cress is a good kid, but she's romantic and, you know, a kid can get carried away—"

"Yeah. Well, what can you tell me about Richie Darden?"

"Not much. I think he came originally from California. He just walked in here one night, with a guitar, and the first thing I knew, he was up there singing, which he was very good at, and then later we put him on a regular spot. About two weeks, I think."

"Did you get acquainted with him at all?"

"No—I see so many—"

"No history on him?"

"Nobody seemed to know him, and he wasn't talkative about himself."

"Is he good? Special?"

"Well—they liked him. To be honest with you, I'm a businessman, and this is a pretty good business, so far. If you can bring them in, you're good."

"Does it take a musician to judge?"

"Oh no—you see, it doesn't have much to do with music. I think what you have to be is seventeen, eighteen years old—at heart, anyway. It's the song, you see, and how you come by it and how you sing it, how much heart you can put in it. That's how I see it, anyway. Leave it to them—the kids know the difference. We get along fine. I tell you—some of these kids will break your heart."

"How old is Richie Darden?"

"I don't know—older than the kids. I'd say twenty-four, twenty-five. Of course, as a performer, you can be a hundred years old and still cut it, if you have the heart."

"Have you heard from Richie, or anything about him, since he left here?"

"No. Doesn't Cress know where he is?"

"No, she says she doesn't."

"Well—oh, yeah, the other day I heard—he showed up at a hootenanny, in Champaign—university crowd. Somebody here had a clipping—"

"I beg your pardon," I said. "'Hootenanny'?"

"Yes, that's a gathering of folk singers and dancers—they get together and do whatever they can do, eat hot dogs and so on, have a real ball."

"Champaign? When was this?"

"I'm not sure, couple of weeks ago."

He glanced down at the shambles of the spotlight at his feet, dropped his cigarette to the floor and stepped on it.

"Could you do something for Cress?" I asked.

"Sure."

"She's worried about Richie coming back and not being able to find her at the apartment. Can we keep in touch with you, so you can put him in touch with us?"

"Sure. Where are you now?"

"Around town. We'll drop you a line now and then."

"Okay. Say, about those three—whatever they are—if they turn up here—"

"Call the cops," I said. "You may use my name."

"That serious?"

"I guess so. Thanks for the talk."

"Don't mention it."

I started down the steps and he came after me.

"Listen," he said, "I just thought of something—if you're interested in the singing—"

"Yes," I said.

"You can tell when you cry," he said.

I looked at him.

"I mean it," he said. "Take a song like—'Barbara Allen'—been sung deep into the ground and back again. Everybody does it. Well, somebody starts singing it and you think, 'My God, not again!' and like as not, when it's finished, you'll feel the same way. But once in a while somebody you never heard before will start it and the first thing you know, you're listening, and before it's finished, you're crying. That's the way I can tell, and I think that's how the kids do it, too."

"Could Richie Darden do it?" I asked. "Make you cry?"

"Not me. But he did it for a lot of them. I saw it happen."

"Okay, thanks for the tip. I'll let you know when I cry."

"Do that," he said. "Give my best to Cress."

I went on down and left the place and drove around the corner. I crossed the street to her apartment building, which in the full light of day looked dingier than at night, though still better than the newer housing project.

I'm getting old, I thought.

Inside it wasn't much different from the night, except that there was more sound: slamming of doors, occasional voices. I didn't meet anyone in the hall, or on the stairs, going up. On the third floor I saw that the door of her apartment was open and an elderly man with noticeable arthritis was sweeping with a large broom, from inside of the room out into the hall. He had a couple of cartons out there, a dustpan and other paraphernalia.

I walked down the hall and waited till he saw me standing outside the door.

"Nobody home?" I said. "I'm looking for the Dardens. Richie Darden?"

"Moved out," he said.

"Oh. Suddenly?"

He peered at me over the end of the broom handle.

"Don't know as it was," he said, "don't know as it wasn't. Come up here—everything moved out. Except a pile of trash."

"I know how it is," I said. "Rental units are a headache."

"You can say that again," he said.

I didn't bother. I looked into the cartons and in one of them he had dumped the stack of newspapers that had been on the closet shelf.

"Say," I said, "do you have any use for those old newspapers?"

"Hell, no," he said.

"I could make a hit with my boy if I took them home," I said. "They're running a paper drive, you know? Boy Scouts."

"If you can carry 'em downstairs," he said, "you can have 'em."

"Gee, thanks," I said.

I scooped up the papers and got out of there, not looking back.

In the car I stacked them as neatly as possible and ran through them. They were from half a dozen towns in Indiana and Illinois, north and west of Indianapolis, south and east of Springfield. They dated back about eight weeks, and there were none more recent than a month previous. Most of them, in a consecutive file of about twelve issues, were from a town called Fairmont, Indiana. There were two or three issues each from the other towns. I leafed through them hurriedly. Nothing had been clipped from them and no items had been marked in any way. When I had gone through the stack, I took them to the back of the car and put them in the trunk.

* * * *

At the hotel I let myself into my own room quietly. The connecting door was barely ajar and I heard guitar strumming in her room. I stood listening as she played, by fits and starts, feeling something out, looking for something on the instrument. She struck a couple of deep chords, then fingered her way lightly up and down the scale. Her voice came, quavering, searching like her fingers. I couldn't make out the words at first. Suddenly all the sound ceased. She cleared her throat, strummed one solid chord, and her voice rose slightly. She sang:

> *You can't be sure;*
> *Don't say you're sure—*
> *Only of death and taxes.*

It stopped again abruptly. I tiptoed to the door, opened it and closed it with a slight, firm bang. I started across the room and the connecting door swung open slowly.

"Is that you—Mac?" she said.

"Yes, it's me."

She came in slowly, dragging the guitar behind her. She was wearing pedal pushers and a loose blouse and her hair tumbled gold around her face in the light behind her.

CHAPTER FIVE

"Did you see Roger?" she asked.

"Yes. I promised to keep in touch with him."

One finger twanged one string on the guitar, whether with purpose or by accident, I couldn't tell.

"Did he...?" she said. "Did he say whether he...?"

"Heard from Richie?" I said. "No, he hasn't."

She turned away, lifted the guitar to the bed and sat beside it, slumping.

"How did things go here?" I asked.

"All right," she said.

"Did you have something to eat?"

She shook her head.

"Nothing? All day?"

"No—I wasn't hungry."

"Cress—"

She flared in sudden anger, snappy as a cigarette lighter.

"Well," she said, "I called on the phone and I couldn't understand what the man said even. How could I tell him anything?"

"Oh," I said.

As clearly as if it were happening again, I remembered myself, a kid, on the telephone in a tenement hallway, trying to order something from Mr. Cohen's delicatessen, because my mother was sick in bed and didn't want me to leave her. Mr. Cohen had a heavy accent and I couldn't understand him, so naturally I was certain I couldn't get through to him. I remembered my quick fury and slamming the receiver onto the hook and standing there in a rage of defeat. I couldn't remember what happened about the order, but the feelings all came back—the anger, the black frustration, the hatred of Mr. Cohen.

"I'm sorry you had that problem," I said. "Some of these people don't speak up very plain."

"It's all right," she said. "Who cares?"

"Well, I care if you go hungry. Give me a minute to wash up and we'll get a meal."

I left abruptly, to cut off the lingering strains of the *pathétique*. While I freshened up, I confronted a certain concern just beginning to assert itself. I had been carried along by the necessity of handling an urgent, immediate problem. Now I had done what I could about that, and what stretched ahead seemed more harrowing, partly because it was unknowable. But what was knowable provided small comfort. Cress was a minor female, a subhuman vertebrate, subject to specific laws and not subject to ordinary understanding, even under ideal conditions. The only secure place for a minor female, I decided, was home.

She must have had a home, I thought. She had to come from somewhere.

"Where were you born, Cress?" I asked, across the dinner table.

She couldn't answer right away because she had a mouthful of mashed potatoes. I had brought her to a cafeteria in the hope that the vast array of food would stimulate her appetite. It had worked quite well, except that some of her choices had puzzled me: the combination, for instance, of the potatoes and macaroni.

"Where was I born?"

"Yes. In Chicago?"

"No, in a little town."

I let a minute pass.

"Well," I said, "every town has a name."

"What difference does it make?" she said. "I'm never going back there."

"Nobody there anymore?" I said. "Place all boarded up?"

She gave me a narrow look.

"Not exactly," she said. "My mother's there—and my sister."

"You don't ever want to see them?"

"I don't care," she said. "The thing is, they don't want to see me."

We seemed to be heading down by *Uncle Tom's Cabin* again, so I dropped it for the time being.

"Where did Richie Darden come from?" I asked.

"California."

"Los Angeles?"

"Hollywood. You want all the details?"

"I would appreciate it, yes."

"He graduated from Hollywood High School in 1956. He was in the army for two years. He was married to a girl named Susan and they were divorced in 1960. He lived on Fountain Avenue with his mother and father and a dog named Shep. He started playing the guitar when he was in the army and he appeared at the Ash Grove in Hollywood in 1961 and went on the road, and he came to Chicago about four months ago and that's when I first met Richie Darden."

"That's very good," I said. "What does he look like? What color eyes does he have?"

"You saw his picture—"

"In black and white. I was wondering about his complexion."

"Very nice."

"Very nice what?"

"Nice complexion," she said.

"His hair black—dark eyes?"

"I guess so."

"What would you like for dessert?" I asked.

That shook her some.

"Dessert? We were talking about Richie—"

"Yes, but I notice you cleaned up your plate in good style. Maybe you'd like something more."

"Uh—coffee?" she said.

"Coffee it is. Cream and sugar?"

"Black—please," she said.

I went for the coffee, and when I got back to the table, she was smoking a cigarette in that dedicated, meticulous way she had.

"What is Richie like to live with?" I asked.

Over the rim of her coffee cup her eyes probed at me, not without malice.

"You want all the details about that, too?" she said.

"I was thinking about his personality. Is he a happy, relaxed fellow, or does he get moody, depressed?"

She gave this some serious attention.

"Well—he would sometimes get low in his mind. But he doesn't stay that way. I can always snap him out of it."

"When he would get low in his mind, did he ever say why? Was there something troubling him?"

Our interests in Richie Darden were not interlocking.

"He had this song, see, one of his favorites—'Lonesome Train'—and whenever he would get low that way, I would sing it to him:

Ain't gonna ride that lonesome train,
Ain't gonna ride that train no more;
Had all of that lonesome train I need:
Lonesome train—
Lonesome train…whoo-eee-oo!

"You see, when Richie sings it, he makes that sound like a train whis-tle—lonesome and far-off sounding—and I can't do it like he can, so when I get to that part, it makes him laugh. And I can always snap him out of it, singing that song."

"Then he snaps right out of it, huh?"

"Yes, he does. Of course, there are other ways. But that's none of your business."

"All right. Shall we get out of here?"

She finished her coffee and snuffed out the cigarette.

"Mac—do we have to stay in that hotel?"

"Certainly not," I said. "But why do you ask? Are you afraid there?"

"Not exactly…"

"Is it because of me? Because we're sharing accommodations?"

She laughed suddenly.

"Oh no! I'm not afraid of *you!*"

"You're not?"

"Besides—I'm not that much of a square."

"I don't know that I like it too well that you're not afraid of me," I said, "but I'm glad you're not a complete square—whatever that is. What is it about the hotel that bugs you?"

She wriggled over it with creased brow, shrugged and shook her head.

"I can't explain it. It's a bad feeling—like I'm closed up in there and something's going to happen and I don't know what."

"All right. What I had in mind was that we would take a short trip and see if we can find a hootenanny."

"A hoot—? Where? Tonight?"

"Probably not tonight, but they had one awhile back down at Cham-paign."

"Where's that?"

"Down south a little. Where the university is."

"Then let's go."

* * * *

It was a three-block walk to the hotel and she set a brisk pace, long, slender legs driving, her hands swinging free.

The smell of trouble was in my nose like a bad breath as we crossed the threshold to the lobby, but it hadn't blown soon enough, and even if it had, there would have been no way to avoid it. It took the form of two police officers, one male, the other female. I didn't know them. The male partner identified himself and asked if I were myself and I said yes and he said:

"Come with us, please."

I wanted badly to check with the hotel cop.

"All right," I said, "but could I leave a message at the desk?"

"Rather you didn't," he said. "We've been waiting quite awhile."

I glanced at Cress, whose face had closed the way a night-blooming cereus closes at dawn.

"Everything will be all right," I said.

She showed no panic and no sign of protest, but as we faced about to leave the lobby, she put her mouth to my ear and hissed:

"The suitcase!"

The suitcase was in the trunk of the car, in the hotel garage, where she had insisted we lock it before going to the cafeteria. There was nothing to be done about that either.

"Don't worry," I said. "Everything will be all right."

Surely it will, I thought. What have we done?

Well, a little, I thought. We haven't turned in that gun yet, that I told Sergeant Schnell about, and we more or less shacked up—technically speaking—in a couple of hotel rooms with a minor female, but aside from that—

They wouldn't bother about any of it unless something else happened.

"What happened?" I asked the officer, as he opened the front door of their car and nodded me in.

I got no answer, but I hadn't expected one.

* * * *

It was a short ride. I sat in front with the officer-driver and Cress sat in back with the female officer and nobody said a word to anybody. We left the car at the ambulance entrance of a dilapidated but still functioning receiving hospital, and we all went in there and traversed some crowded corridors to a swinging door marked: *City Emergency.* I had a knotty feeling between my shoulder blades.

The officer pushed at the door and I halted as he glanced at me.

"Easy," I said. "What is the girl expected to confront here?"

He held his reply for a count of three.

"It's all been cleaned up," he said. "How old is she?"

"Eighteen," I said.

"Well—let's get it over with," he said.

It was a ward, containing a row of beds along each of the two long walls, and at the far end, six narrow, more or less private one-bed cubicles. Curtains were drawn around some of the beds in the two rows, about half of which were occupied. The curtains were some comfort, but there were several exposed accident cases and there was a good deal of audible suffering and it was not a pleasant place to be. I looked around to see how Cress was taking it, and she was walking along firmly, her eyes cast down, her face still closed.

We made the full run between the rows of beds and came to the second cubicle from the left. Sergeant Schnell came out of it and nodded to the other officers—not to me—and looked at Cress with curiosity. The other male officer gestured to me and we went in there.

In the high hospital bed lay a man, heavily bandaged about the face and head. There were openings for his eyes, nose and mouth, and that was about all you could see of him. On a chair beside the bed, her right hand holding his left, sat a young woman in slacks and a white blouse, wearing large horn-rimmed glasses. It was the girl I had seen at The Mill.

"Roger?" I said, to nobody in particular.

The officer didn't say anything and the girl in the glasses looked at me from a tired, empty face.

"Two men jumped him," the officer said, "in the alley behind his place of business. We'd like some identification."

I moved along the bed, across from where the woman was sitting.

"This is his wife, Mrs. Semple," the officer said.

We looked at each other across the mound Roger made on the bed. I couldn't read her mind, but she had seen me visit her husband that afternoon and a few hours later he had been badly beaten, so the conclusions among which she could choose were limited.

"I'm sorry," I said.

I was saying it to both of them, but only Roger replied. His voice was muffled by the bandages and his right eye looked at me. The left eye wasn't much good to him.

"Like you said," he said, "I should have called the police. But—didn't really have time."

Cress had moved into the room and was standing at the foot of the bed.

"Hello, Mrs. Semple," she said.

"Hello, Cress."

"Roger?" Cress said.

"Hi, Cress," Roger said. "You all right?"

"Yes. I'm all right."

"There were two of them?" I said.

"I guess so," Roger said. "Felt like an army—but I think there were two."

"One of them had black hair, very low across his forehead?"

"Uh—yeah, from what I could see. Not much light out there."

Sergeant Schnell was leaning against the wall near the entrance to the room, his face impassive. The other officer was behind me, listening. The policewoman stood a little way off from Cress at the foot of the bed.

"What did they talk about?" I asked Roger. "I mean, they didn't just start in on you without a word, did they?"

"No—oh no," he said. "They asked—they wanted to know where Richie Darden was. And I said I didn't know—he was on the road and I hadn't heard from him."

He shifted carefully under the bed cover. Mrs. Semple got up and put her hand on his head.

"Then," he said, "they asked where they could find Cress. And I said I didn't know. But they didn't believe me. They said—you must have told me. I said no—but they wouldn't accept that—and then they started in."

There was a minute of dead silence. Mrs. Semple looked along the bed toward Schnell.

"Enough now?" she said in a flat, dead voice. "Can I take him to a regular hospital now?"

"Yes, ma'am," Schnell said, pushing away from the wall. "Let's go," he said.

"I'm sorry," I said to Roger.

"No—not your fault," he said.

"Yes, I should have given you something to tell them."

He lifted his hand and dropped it on the bed. I looked at his wife, but she was looking at something else.

We moved out of the ward in a ragged recessional, Sergeant Schnell, then me, then the other officer and, behind us, Cress with the policewoman. Outside, under the sign that read "Ambulance Only," the three officers bunched together momentarily and left Cress and me alone. I felt her fingers against the back of my hand.

"It was like a movie," she said. "Roger—with all those bandages. Like one of those war movies."

"It wasn't a movie, Cress," I said.

Her hand left me. The policewoman came over.

"Do you want to come to the car with me, Cress?" she said.

"Go ahead, Cress," I said.

They walked over to the car and got into the back seat. Sergeant Schnell and the other officer came to me.

"You said the girl is eighteen?" the officer asked.

"Yeah," I said.

They looked at each other.

"Statutory offense?" Schnell said.

The other shrugged.

They knew she wasn't eighteen. They also knew they weren't sure what to do about her. They were up against a situation they had to take cognizance of, but they had no complaint to act on, except for the thing about Roger. Schnell knew I had at least a tenuous involvement there and he wanted to get at me, but the girl was obviously under my protection and they had to make some provision for her.

"I'll cooperate as far as I can," I said, "but I'm not going to do your work for you. I can't tell you any more about those two slugs than I have already. I heard they're from out of town and that's about it."

They hung over me in silence, like a couple of scavenger birds at dusk.

"As for the girl," I said, "she's my client. If you want to come to the hotel and look at the setup, it's all right with us. It's about as sanitary as I know how to make it under the circumstances."

"Yeah," Schnell said. "It's those circumstances that got us worried."

"I'm a little worried myself," I said.

"You mentioned a suitcase," Schnell said.

"Well," I said, "all our luggage is at the hotel."

"All right," he said. "Here we go."

He walked away and I went along with the other officer to the car where Cress was waiting with the policewoman. Schnell had stopped and was looking back at us.

"I think Sergeant Schnell would like you to ride with him," the officer said.

"No," I said. "If that's the way you want it, you'll have to make your move now. I stay with the girl till you make an official separation."

He subjected me to brief study. I was on fairly thin ice, but they weren't exactly on dry land. Finally he waved at Schnell, the two of us got into the front seat of the car, and we headed downtown.

CHAPTER SIX

We entered the hotel by a side door and got up to our suite without causing noticeable embarrassment to the management. The officers gave the accommodations a cursory inspection. I watched the policewoman exchange looks with the other two officers and saw how, without saying anything, they made a decision to pass over the matter of the private eye and the minor female. Schnell, however, was left with unfinished business on his hands.

"I guess you could get on with your chores," he said to the others. "I'll talk to these people awhile."

The policewoman and the other officer left and Cress and I sat down with Schnell.

"Miss," he said to Cress, "what did this Richie Darden have that these two characters want so bad?"

"I don't know," Cress said.

"Well, do you know where Richie Darden is at this time?"

"No, I don't."

"What was he—kind of your boyfriend?"

"Kind of," she said.

"He was one of these—a folk singer?"

"One of the best."

"Well, miss, what did he do in his spare time, that you know of?"

"We did all kinds—I mean, he would go to the beach, and the zoo; he would go downtown and walk around and look at the people—"

"What I had more in mind," Schnell said, "Who were his friends? Did he go out with other fellas, play cards, have a few drinks, things like that?"

"No," she said, "he was either alone or with me."

"No other girls?"

"No."

"How long have you known him?"

"Four months."

Schnell looked at me. I tried to indicate with my face that I would help him if I could. I don't know whether he got the message or not.

"Before you knew him, miss," Schnell asked, "what did this Richie Darden do?"

"The same thing. He sang songs and played the guitar."

"I mean where? Where did he come from?"

"California."

"Do you know about any of his associates in California?"

"No. The same as here, I guess," she said.

"Did he ever talk to you about it—about where he'd been, what he did, before he met you?"

"Oh, sure, he talked about a lot of things. Some things he made up songs about."

"Well, now, maybe that would help us. Can you remember any of those songs?"

"I remember all of them. Shall I get my guitar?"

Schnell looked frightened.

"No, no, that won't be necessary—the words is the main thing. What were the songs about?"

"Oh—cowboy songs, songs he made up about the army—"

"Dirty songs?"

"I never heard him sing any dirty songs."

"Well, there's one of these folk songs about Dillinger, for instance. John Dillinger."

"I know that song. Richie never sang it. He didn't like it."

"Did he sing other songs about crooks—gangsters, grifters, people like that?"

"No."

Momentarily at a loss for questions, Schnell took a turn around the room. His hand brushed at my suitcase, on the rack near the bed. He turned from it, went to the connecting door, which was ajar, and pushed it wide open and stood gazing into Cress's room. Cress looked at me without expression and I tried to smile up some strength in her—not that she appeared to need any.

Schnell spoke from the connecting doorway.

"Will you make it tough for me if I look over your luggage?" he said.

"Nope," I said. "Go ahead."

"I could go get a warrant and all that—baloney."

"Don't bother," I said.

He went on inside her room and Cress got out of her chair and slid across to me on her knees, her face no longer impassive, but strained and anxious. Crouching catlike, she appealed to me with her eyes, nose and mouth.

"What does he want with us?" she said.

"He has this problem of who beat up Roger," I said. "He has to solve it if he can and find the men who did it. He knows we were involved with the same men—very likely the same."

"Well, we don't know where they are—or who or anything."

"I know, but he's looking for a lead, anything he can find."

"In our luggage?"

"Anywhere."

She gripped my knee with one hand and I could feel her nails digging like the teeth of a saw.

"Listen," she hissed, "don't let him open Richie's suitcase—"

"Well, Cress—"

"No, please, promise me!" she pleaded.

"But why does it make all that difference?"

"Because I promised Richie!"

"Maybe he won't think of checking the car," I said.

"Even if he does…"

"If I hold out on him, he'll make it hard for us."

"All right!"

"They'll put you in juvenile hall maybe…"

"I'll go there—I'll go to jail."

"Cress—"

"I'm not kidding. I will!"

I put my hand on hers.

Goddamit, I thought, what kind of a promise is that—not to open a suitcase? I don't know how to steer Schnell off it without raising more problems than it may solve…

"Listen," she said, "I hired you, didn't I?"

"Yes…"

"I'll give you the money again—I'll get a job and get more money. You're working for me, aren't you?"

"Yes…"

"Just like a lawyer, or doctor."

"Yes, but even a lawyer—"

"All right! Don't let him open that suitcase."

Luckily I had no chance to reply. Schnell came back. He looked curiously at Cress on her knees but didn't make anything of it. She got up and started into her room.

"Miss—" Schnell said.

"I have to be excused!" she snapped.

"Oh," he said, embarrassed.

She slammed the connecting door between us. Schnell looked at the door, then at me.

"Girls," he said.

"Uh-huh," I said.

"Thank God mine are all grown up now."

"How many do you have?"

"Six."

"Six girls?"

"Yeah. Holy mackerel! I was in hock for ten years, just getting 'em married!"

"All turned out all right?"

"Well—all but one, my oldest. She married this damn bum—a musician. You know, a musician doesn't work but once in a while."

"What instrument does he play?"

"A horn. Some kind of a horn. But he don't play it very often, and he don't know how to do anything else. They're always broke, always scrappin'."

"That's the way it goes."

"Yeah. Look, Mac, what did you have in mind?"

"About what?"

"About this Richie Darden and the girl and all. I mean, what did you have in mind to do about it?"

I went through the outward motions of giving it some thought, vain though I knew it was.

"The exact truth is," I said, "I'm not sure. The main thing I have in mind is to get in touch with Richie Darden and get lined out on the situation. Then about the girl, I'll have to see what happens at the time."

"What do you think the situation is? You must have some theory. What does the girl tell you?"

"Just what she told you. No more than that."

"This Richie Darden—"

"He is a mystery man to me," I said. "He and Cress had a thing together and as far as I can tell, it was a good thing. She loves him."

"You think he was pushing something on the side and the girl was in on it with him?"

"I don't have any idea whether he was or not, but I'm certain she wasn't in it with him."

"What makes you so sure? Because she paid you?"

"No—she did pay me. But I believe her. Basically I believe what she says."

"I don't believe her," he said stubbornly.

"Well, that's your trade; disbelief. I didn't believe her at first, but I came around."

"I think maybe we get out a bulletin on this Richie Darden."

"How can you? What do you want him for?"

"Questioning."

I shrugged.

"All right. If I find him first, I'll ask him some questions of my own."

Schnell stabbed his thumb over his shoulder toward the other room.

"In that suitcase in there," he said, "that knife—"

"I asked her about that. It's his knife, but she says she never saw it before."

"She shouldn't carry it around like that."

"I know. I'll get rid of it."

"That gun you took away from the hoodlums."

I nodded toward my suitcase on the rack. Schnell went through it at some length, but I had a feeling he was only going through the motions.

"What did you learn from that third guy, the one we found in the catalogue?"

I told him, but I left it out about the telephone call, because there wouldn't be anything he could do about that now and I was afraid he would be upset that I didn't call him in on it.

He found the gun and examined it thoroughly and put it in his pocket.

"You have your own?" he asked.

"Yes," I said.

"What for?"

"I've got the necessary papers."

"Don't get touchy."

"All right."

"She had a bunch of songs, wrote out on music paper, in the suitcase," he said.

"Yes."

"Is that what Richie Darden left with her that's so important?"

"I don't know. It could be. A folk singer's stock in trade is his songs. It could be worth plenty."

"To a couple of slugs?"

"It doesn't seem likely."

It could be in the other suitcase, I was thinking. He might have had some numbers in there he hadn't got around to protecting yet and he might have told her not to open it, because if they got out and around, they might be lifted. It just could be. But then, why wouldn't he tell her? Because he couldn't trust her not to let her woman's curiosity get the better of her. It might be that kind of thing.

Schnell was grumbling.

"Always gettin' in trouble, makin' trouble," he said. "Goddam beatniks—"

"Let's distinguish among beatniks," I said. "Folk singing has an ancient, honorable history. Carl Sandburg, Burl Ives…"

He grunted in mild bewilderment. He moved heavily around the room, as if he wanted to leave and couldn't think of a good tag line.

"Well," he said, "I'll check out the rest of it and get on my way. Where's your car?"

He had thought of the line all right, a good, snappy one.

"In the hotel garage," I said.

"You want to come along with me, or you want to give me the keys?"

"The keys are with the attendant," I said.

Cress, I thought, I don't know what else to do.

Maybe he won't insist on opening it, I thought.

Oh yes, he will, I thought.

"The girl better come with us," he said.

"She'll be all right for a few minutes," I said.

Part of my trouble was that I wanted to see the inside of that suitcase almost as much as Schnell did, and I didn't want Cress to know about it if we could avoid it.

"Is that the way you take care of your clients?" he asked. "Leave 'em alone in a hotel?"

"Knock it off," I said.

He marched to the connecting door with his hand outstretched.

"Knock!" I said.

He hesitated, then rapped briskly with his knuckles. I heard Cress's voice. By then I had joined him and he opened the door carefully and looked in. I looked over his shoulder. She was coming from the bathroom, closing the door behind her.

I hope she isn't sick, I thought. What if she gets sick?

"Cress," I said, "Sergeant Schnell wants to check out the car."

She looked at me and at him and shrugged.

"You want me to go, too?" she said.

"If you don't mind," Schnell said.

"All right," she said. "Let me get my sweater."

She got a sweater out of the closet and put it over her shoulders and we went out to the elevator. Nothing was said while we waited. On the way down to the garage Schnell asked her:

"You know what 'pot' is, miss?"

"Yes," she said.

"You ever use any yourself?"

"No."

"Anything else along that line?"

"No."

"Did Richie Darden ever use it that you know of?"

"No, not that I know of."

At the garage level we got out and went over to the attendant's office to get the keys. Cress hung back in the shadows, waiting.

"Going out, sir?" the attendant asked.

"No, not yet," I said. "Just want to look for something."

He gave us the keys and we went to the car. Cress followed us at some distance and stood with her arms folded under the loosely draped sweater. Her face was long and mournful looking, but she wasn't chewing her fingernails.

Probably figuring out how to get rid of a private eye, I thought. How to fire a lawyer.

The car doors were unlocked, and Schnell opened the front door to get light and looked into the car. He didn't linger over it.

"Open the trunk," he said.

I looked at Cress and shrugged. She looked back at me from a stony face. I stuck the key in the slot, twisted and let the trunk lid swing up. Schnell took a look and grunted softly. There was nothing in the trunk but a few tools and an old raincoat of mine.

"Okay," he grunted.

I closed the trunk and we walked with him out to the street.

"If you get a lead on Richie Darden," he said.

"Yes," I said.

"Be careful," he said. "Good night. Good night, miss."

Cress said nothing.

"So long, Sergeant," I said.

We stood there on the drafty street until he had disappeared around the corner of the building. Then we walked back through the garage to the attendant's office and left the keys. Our footsteps echoed on the concrete floor.

We got in the elevator and started up.

"What did you do with the suitcase?" I asked.

"I put it in the bathroom," she said.

"You made good time."

She had nothing to say for the next fifteen minutes. We stayed in our separate rooms, closed off from each other, even though the connecting door stood ajar. I moved around some, but as far as I know, she sat on the edge of the bed and watched the time go by in that special world inside her head.

I wonder what it's like in there, I thought. What does she think about? What images does she have?

Eventually I got a partial answer. She called to me. I went to the door and stood there, and she was sitting on the bed with her hands hanging between her knees.

"You would have let him open it," she said.

"I don't know," I said. "I think so."

"Why?"

"Because he was a police officer with a job to do and there was no way to prevent it without getting into problems."

"You afraid of problems?"

"Not for myself."

"For me?"

"Cress, do you know what it's like in juvenile hall?"

"I don't care what it's like."

"All right."

Her fists clenched and relaxed and she looked at them vaguely, as if they belonged to someone else.

"Would it make it easier for you," I asked, "if I resign? I'll stick around till you find someone else—"

"No," she said. "No—help me."

There was a knock at the door. I opened up and it was the hotel detective.

"Excuse me," I said to Cress, and went out with him.

"You have to throw us out?" I said.

"Well, the fellows from downtown were here."

"Yeah. They're gone now."

"I know it. But the management is worried—about the whole situation."

"Okay," I said, "we'll check out."

"You know how it is—"

"Sure."

"Listen, there were a couple of others hanging around."

"Recently?"

"Last half hour. Down around the garage. The attendant figured they were after a car—he lost one last week; left the office for a couple of minutes and whamm-o! So naturally he was nervous and he called me. By the time I got down there, they were gone."

"He give you a description?"

"Not much. Hard-looking guys."

How the hell did they pick up the hotel? I thought. Of course, with all that activity back and forth—if they kept track of Roger Semple, they could have kept track of us from there on.

"Thanks for the news," I said. "I'm sorry if we got you in trouble."

"No trouble yet," he said. "But the boss just called me in and asked how long you planned to stay."

"I got it. Thanks again. Take it easy."

"Any time I can, Mac."

He went away and I went back into the room.

"I guess we'll get going," I said. "All right?"

"All right," she said. "Who was the man?"

"Hotel detective. I asked him to keep an eye on us. So with the police coming around and all, the management got nervous."

"We didn't do anything."

"I know."

"Where will we go?"

"We'll leave town," I said. "We'll hit the road."

She opened her suitcase on the bed and started putting things in it.

CHAPTER SEVEN

It took some time to win back her confidence. We left the hotel at about ten-thirty and I drove at a leisurely pace toward the southwest edge of the city. There had been no sign of the two ugly shadows and I wanted to spot them, if possible, but the traffic was still heavy and I couldn't distinguish them in the parade. I didn't want to get into open country in the middle of the night, when I couldn't find them and didn't know where we were going.

At midnight I began looking for a place to turn in for the night and Cress noticed a coffeehouse. I was very tired, and because she was still angry with me, she didn't say anything except to mention its existence. But I knew she wanted to go in there and we had to start somewhere, so I found a place to park, locked Richie Darden's suitcase in the trunk, gave her the key, and we went into the place, named The Open Grave. There were some weird-looking figures painted in black on a deep-blue background, and the entrance was marked by an arrow cut into a headstone.

The interior was smaller and less pretentious than The Mill. The foyer contained a few records and books for sale, but nobody was browsing in them. There were posters and fliers on the walls, and we studied all of them carefully and found no mention of Richie Darden and no picture that was his likeness. There was an air of sleepiness about the place and the theater section was nearly deserted. We sat down in there, along with the half-dozen other patrons, and a girl in tight black stretch pants brought us a bill of fare. We could have any of twelve kinds of coffee, beer or wine, and soft drinks and fruit juice. But the girl explained the coffee machine had broken down and all they had was regular coffee. We ordered it. I asked if there would be any entertainment and the girl said yes, pretty soon.

"Maybe he'll just walk in here," Cress said, "like he did at The Mill."

"Maybe," I said.

We drank the coffee and ordered some more. Two young men in slacks and sweaters were bent over a chessboard at a nearby table. Some distance away sat a teen-age couple, clinging to each other in silence. Two girls who appeared to be about nineteen were sitting together near the small platform that formed the stage. They wore sweaters and shorts and black stockings and they had long, dark hair down over their shoulders.

"Cress," I said, "it's a big country. Can you think of any place, any town or city, Richie ever mentioned?"

She looked at me helplessly.

"I don't know…" she said. "Maybe he went back to California."

"Then why would he leave the suitcase with you?"

"I don't know."

"Did he say when he'd be back?"

"He said in a couple of weeks. He said he couldn't drag the suitcase along with him and he left it with me to take care of."

"How long has he been gone now?"

"About three weeks."

"Did he leave all of a sudden? Did he make plans in advance? How did he take his leave?"

"Well—he just—one night we came home from The Mill and he said, 'Cress, I've got to go away for a while. I'll be back.'"

"Did you ask him any questions about it? Where he was going?"

"I asked him if I could go, too, and he said no. And I asked him where he was going and he said there were some places he wanted to visit, to pick up some songs he'd heard about."

"He didn't say where?"

"No. But he said only a couple of weeks, so I thought he was just go-ing—maybe as far as Kentucky or Tennessee."

"Did Richie have a car?"

"No—not then. He said he was going on the bus. He gave me some money and told me to take care of the suitcase and not to open it or let anyone else open it, and then he picked up his guitar and a little traveling bag he had and he left."

"You said he didn't have a car—'not then.' Did he have one before?"

"When I first met him he had a car, but then he decided he didn't need it around Chicago and it was too expensive to keep up, so one day he sold it."

"Were you with him when he sold it?"

"No. He came home and told me he'd sold it."

"What kind of car was it?"

"Oh, just a car—ordinary car, about two years old. We used to take a ride in it once in a while, up to Milwaukee, or around town. Once we drove to some place in Michigan and back. It took all day and all night."

"But when he left, he said he was going by bus?"

"Yes."

"Did he mention any people—did he ever mention any names of people he'd known?"

"Yes, he knew a lot of people, but I don't remember the names."

"None at all? Was there anyone special—anyone he mentioned more than the others?"

"I can't remember—yes, there was a man named Duffy—Clare Duffy."

"What did he say about him?"

"Well, he just said this person was a good friend of his and meant more to him even than his own father."

"Somebody in California?"

"No, he lives here somewhere—I mean, not in Chicago, but down in the state somewhere. Richie knew him in the army, but he was about to retire from the army. He was a regular army man, a sergeant, I think."

"You don't remember where Richie said he lived?"

"No."

Some lights flashed and three more young people came in, separately, and took seats here and there. After about two minutes one of the two boys at the chessboard made a move, rose from his chair and picked up a guitar which was lying against the wall near the stage. He hung it over his shoulder and walked around, tuning it. His chess partner made a move and the guitar player went to the table and studied the board, twanging his strings absently, made his move and walked away. He stopped beside the two girls sitting near the stage, leaned over and conversed with them for a couple of minutes. Then he mounted the stage and, without announcement, started to sing.

"He's a phony!" Cress hissed.

"How do you know?" I asked.

"He's just filling in for somebody and he doesn't know what he's doing."

I tried to listen to the song. It was a political song with some pretty good lines, but it didn't punch out much. It sounded like that day's *Chicago Tribune* editorial turned inside out and set to music. Or maybe it was the way the young man did it, as Cress had suggested.

When he finished there was a polite smattering of applause. The guitar player nodded an acknowledgment and went over to the chess board. He made a move rather quickly and said loudly, "Check." Then he looked at the two girls, who giggled.

"Oh, God," Cress said gloomily.

One of the recent newcomers in the house was a tall, muscular Negro, who sat near us, very quiet and patient looking. Cress began to take notice of him, but he took no evident notice of her. The guitar player got up and started another song, an old ballad about one of the queens of England. Even I remembered it, once he got started. He sang it well, I thought. He had a rich, true voice that had obviously had some training, and he had a pleasant, unobtrusive manner. When he finished this one, Cress curled her lip.

"Very pretty," she sneered.

I glanced around and the Negro boy had heard her and was smiling. When he saw me looking at him, he stopped smiling. I nodded to him but got no response.

The boy sang another tune and this one went over somewhat better. He got a nice reception when he finished, except for Cress.

"That's a good song," she said. "Too bad he has to ruin it."

"Well," I said, "he seems to know all the words."

She gave me a look, then her shoulder. The waitress brought the Negro a cup of coffee and lingered, talking to him in a low voice. His white teeth flashed at her.

"Jocko!" the guitar player said loudly, "sing something!"

Everyone turned and looked at the Negro, who had stopped smiling, disconcerted by the sudden attention. Applause broke out and I heard the waitress say:

"Go ahead, Jocko."

The guitar player stepped down, offering his instrument. With what seemed to be honest reluctance, the Negro got up and accepted it.

"Now…!" Cress said under her breath.

Two bright spots of color glowed in her long, pale face.

"You've heard him before?" I said.

She gave me another look.

"He's bound to have something to sing about," she said.

I had to agree on the general principle, but I didn't see how she could know merely by looking at him that he would be able to deliver it.

Surely, I thought, in stubborn skepticism, there are Negroes who *can't* sing with unusual distinction.

As it turned out, this boy sang with a lot of power and style. I had never heard the songs before. They were original and gutsy and he sang them, as near as I could judge, from the heart. Considering the size of the audience, his reception was very large.

In the middle of his third number this drunk wandered in. He came in more or less unnoticed. I happened to see him because of my position and possibly because I was less involved in the music than the others. He was standing just inside the door, weaving a little, minding his own business to the extent that a man in his condition can understand what his business is.

After the first glance I stopped paying attention, figuring he would wander out as he had come in.

When the song ended, the applause was enthusiastic and extended, especially by the drunk. Heads turned, including mine, and I saw a stocky man in shirt sleeves confronting the smashed one. I took him to be the manager. On the platform the Negro stood with the guitar, not sure whether to go on or step down. The manager put his hand on the drunk's sleeve, as if to help him make his exit, but the guy pulled free and lumbered down toward the stage. Reaching up with both hands, his fingers spread, he bellowed:

"Gimme that banjo, baby—I'll give you lessons!"

The Negro looked at him and then out over the house. The two chess players stood up at their table, but neither made any move. The manager was coming down the aisle behind the drunk, somewhat warily.

"Gimme that thing…" the drunk babbled.

Clutching the air, he hit the low platform with his knees and sprawled on his face. The Negro boy jumped nimbly out of the way. One of the two girls in the black stockings wasn't so lucky—the drunk's flailing legs knocked her chair out from under her and she went to the floor.

By now the manager had reached the stage. He started to help the girl, who brushed him aside. Then he got hold of the drunk and got him on his feet.

"Lemme have the box, buddy," the drunk said. "Wanna sing to the people."

The manager said something and the drunk pushed him away and glared up over the stage.

"Don' wanna hear a white man sing, huh?" he said. "Just niggers."

This bothered the manager and he took a firm grip on the drunk's arm. This, in turn, bothered the drunk, who lashed out at the manager, knocking him flat. One of the two chess players moved away from the table, but indecisively. All of a sudden the drunk was in a rage. He kicked at the manager's face, missed, and in the follow-through, out of control, swung his fist into the face of one of the chess players, knocking him down.

I left my chair and wrapped my arms around the drunk's waist. We both hit the floor, but well in the clear. He was thrashing around quite a lot and I got disengaged from him, rolled him over, got his hands behind him and gave a tug. He squawked and I eased off on the pressure.

"All right, buddy," I said, "let me give you a hand up."

He was still hot but too disorganized to put up a fight, and he let himself be helped up and propelled to the door. He hung back there, mumbling that he could sing a few "nigger songs" himself if they would just let him have the "banjo." I pushed him on outside.

"Hey, Jack," he mumbled, "lemme back in there long enough to get a little drink, huh? I need it."

"You can't get a drink in there," I said. "It's a coffeehouse. Now go ahead home."

In a kind of blaze, as if looking into a kaleidoscope, I noticed that the people from inside had joined us and figured out that the kaleidoscope effect came from the combined head lamps and spotlight of a cruising police car.

"Oh, hell," I thought.

I slumped against the cold brick wall, between the stupefied citizen and the coffeehouse entrance. We were in a dingy section of a dingy suburb which I knew only by reputation as a "tough town." On my left the manager was saying something I couldn't make out, and beyond him I saw the two chess players. A couple of girls were peering out from the doorway, and I saw the Negro boy push past them and come out to the street.

The patrol car had swung into the curb and two officers in blue suits and white helmets got out. The girls in the doorway disappeared and Cress looked out.

We must have made quite a spectacle, ranged along that wall in various attitudes of perplexity and dishevelment. Even funnier when, just as the officers' boots hit the curb, the drunk decided to cut. He ran in front of me, back toward the entrance, shouldering the manager into the wall. One of the chess players stuck out a foot and tripped him. Then both chess players leaned down to get hold of him and he came up fighting. Along in there the police stepped in.

They were well trained in the manly arts and waded into the scrimmage readily. If it had been a game, they'd have been charged with unnecessary roughness, especially against the two boys, who were just trying to help, but they did get things organized in a hurry.

I made a wide trek around the fringe of the fracas, looking for Cress. I saw her just inside the entrance and had made my way to the threshold when I heard the manager make a sudden, sharp protest.

The cops had everybody racked up against the wall, except for the drunk, who was wandering around on his own. They were going after the two kids and the manager, verbally, threatening to close down the place, talking about troublemakers—the same old police argument. One of the boys started talking back and one of the cops put a hand on his chest and rocked him into the wall. I could hear his head bang against the brick.

"We just about had it from you beatniks," the cop said.

All I wanted to do was to go to bed somewhere.

I left the doorway and stuck a shoulder between the cops and the kids.

"They didn't have anything to do with it," I said. "The drunk came in and made a fuss—"

"Who are you?" one of them said.

His face was a tight mass of jutting bone and angled cartilage, with eyes bored into it.

"I'm a customer," I said. "I happened to be here when the drunk came in—"

"Go over to the car," the cop said. "We'll get to you in a minute."

"No," I said, "right now."

He blinked and a couple of muscles quivered beside his mouth. The manager had joined us near the door.

"Listen," he said, "this man is trying to tell you what happened."

"Shut up," the cop said. "You—get over to the car—

The other cop had moved along the wall and now confronted the Negro boy, who stood very tall and stiff and silent against the wall.

"Go to your telephone," I told the manager. "Dial the police and tell 'em you want to talk to the chief. Keep telling them until they put somebody on. Then tell him, and stay with it."

He started inside.

"Wait a minute," the cop barked.

"Go ahead," I said.

The manager disappeared. I looked along the wall toward the other cop who was facing the Negro.

"He had the least to do with it of anybody," I said.

Maybe this coffeehouse had been a genuine nuisance to them—maybe not. I had no way of knowing. But it seemed clear enough they'd been looking for an excuse to clamp down, and this, to them, appeared to be it. Meanwhile, the drunk was shambling about in a series of eccentric curves, endangering mostly himself. I couldn't see why he didn't take off, but I was glad of it. I stiffened my arm at a respectful distance from the cop's face and pointed.

"That one," I said, "over there. Everything was peaceful inside. Then he came in. So we brought him outside. That is the whole story."

Nothing in the cards said I would get away with this "interference," and I surely would not have, if it had not been for the general unpredictability of the soused. Somehow I had struck a nerve and the drunk reacted. He came in swinging, and as luck would have it, the first connection he made was on the cop's helmet—bang!

That was all it took. The one who got clobbered had to deal with it and his partner stepped in to help him, and while they were at it, the Negro boy, wisely, slipped away into the night.

"It might be just as well," I said to the chess players, "if you'd go back and finish your game, or something."

On their way in one of them looked back to say:

"You handled that real great, Dad. Thanks."

I nodded.

"We were lucky," I said.

They went in. The officers had the drunk subdued and were stowing him in the back seat of their wagon. The manager looked out and I motioned him back inside. Then Cress came out and I would have sent her back, too, but the officers approached from the curb and it was too late. She crept along the wall, found my hand with hers and held on. The officer with the tight face twitched his muscles at me.

"Everything satisfactory now—sir?" he said.

He was deeply burned, and in a way I regretted it, but in another way, the hell with him. What I did not want to be put down as was a champion of the oppressed—or, for that matter, champion of anything.

"I have no beef," I said. "I happened to be here and saw the way it went."

"Oh," he said. "Well, we certainly do appreciate you setting us straight."

He was asking for it, but he would ask till he was purple before he would get it from me. I held my peace. It wasn't too difficult, with Cress's fingernails digging at my palm.

They spent some time looking at her but decided not to make anything out of it. One of them got out a notebook and pencil.

"What's your name?" he asked. "Just for the record."

I told him.

"Address?"

I gave him that.

"Long way from home, aren't you?" he said.

I shrugged.

"Will you be available to testify in this matter, if necessary?"

"Sure," I said.

He snapped his book shut; they went off a little way and consulted, then got in their car. Cress and I stood there till they had swung around the corner and out of sight.

Her hand moved in mine and I squeezed lightly.

"Mac," she said, "I'm sorry I gave you a bad time—back at the hotel."

"Forget it. Let's find some place to lay our weary heads, huh?"

"All right. But come in first—say good night to Mr. Simon, the man that runs the place."

"Okay."

I went inside with her and Mr. Simon was in the foyer, with the two girls in the stockings. The chess players were back at their board and the young boy and girl were still clinging to each other in the dimly lighted theater. The waitress was watching the chess game.

Mr. Simon was full of gratitude.

"Don't know how to thank you," he said. "Those guys have been bugging me for weeks—I think it's a personal thing."

"I'm sorry they gave you the trouble," I said.

"Listen," he said, "I did what you said. I called the cops and kept asking for the chief—"

"Did you ever get him?"

"No. They said—"

I nodded and we said it together:

"He's out of town."

"It's kind of a trick," I said. "The officers don't know but what you do have a line to the chief. Even if you don't, you might stir up enough curiosity around headquarters to make it exasperating for them."

"It's a good trick. Remind me to remember it."

"Don't try it if you're in the wrong," I said. "It can only backfire."

"Sure, sure," he said. "Let me get you a beer, glass of wine, something—"

"No, thanks. We have to be on our way."

Cress was tugging at my hand. I put my head down and she whispered:

"Richie. Ask him about Richie."

"Oh," I said. "We're kind of looking for a folk singer—we heard him uptown awhile back—Richie Darden. Has he ever sung here? Do you know him?"

"I heard Richie Darden," one of the girls said. "He's terrific. It was on the South Side."

"Recently?" I asked.

"About four months ago."

Mr. Simon was trying to get a word in.

"No, I don't know Richie Darden," he said, "but it's interesting you should ask."

I waited.

"Just tonight—a couple of fellows were asking."

"Tonight. A couple of fellows."

"Yes. After you folks came in, while Jocko was singing—just before the trouble started—these two fellows came in. They asked about Richie Darden."

"What did these two fellows look like?" I asked.

"Well, like a couple of sharp characters—older fellows. They looked inside here and then I guess they decided not to come in. Anyway, they disappeared. Then the damn drunk came in and I forgot about them."

"I see," I said. "Well, thanks. We'll be going."

"Thank *you,*" Mr. Simon said. "Come back—any time. Everything on the house."

"All right," I said. "Good night. Watch out for the cops."

"Hah!" he said. "I know how to handle them!"

We went outside and looked up and down the street. We had left the car half a block away and we walked down there past dark store fronts. Cress opened the trunk and the suitcase was all right. She closed it and gave me the key.

"You keep it," she said.

"I appreciate it," I said, "but don't trust me too far."

Helping her into the car, I took another sighting along the street and saw nothing that posed a threat. But the back of my neck tingled as I slid under the wheel.

Around the corner there was still a good deal of traffic on the highway and nothing could be sorted out of it. I drove about three miles and pulled into the grounds of a large motel that showed a lighted "Vacancy" sign. They had two adjoining rooms with a connecting door, and we took our three suitcases in there and locked ourselves in for the night.

Cress didn't say a word about what the manager had told us until we were both ready for bed. I had just crawled in when she came to the doorway and said:

"You think those were the same two that beat up Roger?"

"I don't like to think so, but I guess I do," I said. "Are you afraid?"

"No," she said. "Not anymore."

She came in and sat on the bed. She was wearing the funny bathrobe and some kind of pajama top that looked like flannel, and where the bathrobe gaped, I saw the swell of her small breasts. She looked unreal, remote in time and space.

"One of the girls back there told me Reuben was around somewhere," she said.

"Who is Reuben?"

"Just about the greatest folk singer in the world, that's who," she said.

"He's around Chicago?"

"No—down in the state. She said he was in Springfield last week. She read it in the paper."

"Well, maybe we'll catch up with him. Is that all the name he has?"

"Yes. Just Reuben."

She put her hand on my face.

"Mac—"

"Yes?"

Her hand clenched and her small fist dug at my neck.

"Nothing," she said. "If it weren't for Richie—"

I opened her hand, kissed it and put it in her lap.

"Sure," I said. "We'll remember Richie in our dreams."

"Good night," she said.

She went to her own room, leaving the door open. When she had settled down, I took my gun from under my pillow, checked it to make sure it was in good order, and replaced it. It made an uncomfortable lump to sleep on, but after a while I adjusted to it.

CHAPTER EIGHT

During breakfast in the motel coffee shop, while Cress lingered, I read all the papers I could find, metropolitan and local, with special attention to the amusement pages. I didn't find Richie Darden's name anywhere and I found very little about any other folk singer, or song or record.

"How come?" I asked Cress.

"I know," she said, "the disc jockeys don't play it, and the coffeehouses don't advertise much. They can't afford it. If there's a big concert, or a real big name—like Reuben—maybe then."

"Why?" I asked.

"It's not commercial," she said. "And some people think it's—what do you call it—touchy?"

"Controversial?"

"Yes. On account of the Freedom Riders and stuff like that."

"When did you first get interested in it?"

"Well, when I was in school, there was this teacher, and he used to sing folk songs. He gave me my first guitar lessons."

"So the coffeehouse was a natural place for you to go when you came to Chicago."

"Yes."

She came to the end of what she had to say about that. I tried to get her to eat something more, but she wouldn't.

I had seen no sign of the two on our tail and let myself hope they had gone off on an independent search. I didn't worry about them at the moment because we were still in the thickly populated outskirts of the city, it was broad daylight and they would be unlikely to mount any shenanigans under those circumstances.

We left the motel, drove to a local telephone office and went through the directories. They had a good supply, including all the metropolitan books and a good many for the outlying communities. There were plenty of "Duffy's" listed but no "Clare Duffy." I found a couple of "C. Duffy's" and dialed both of them, but neither was the ex-sergeant Richie had spoken about.

"I think Richie said he owned a farm," Cress said.

"In Illinois? Indiana?"

"I'm not sure."

In a service station, to persuade myself that we had some plan and were not merely wandering, I plotted a course on a road map. Working crisscross and from north to south, I traced a network of routes downstate, circling each county seat. I found the town of Fairmont, Indiana, and worked it out so that our route would wind up in that general direction and we would cross the line deep in the state.

By lunch time we had made three county seats, all in the northern, thickly settled part of the state, and had turned up nothing from any telephone directory, newspaper, or oral inquiry. In the smaller towns there was no such thing as a coffeehouse. But we found at least one in each of the county seats and nobody had heard anything of Richie Darden. He was totally unknown in two of the places and some people who were hanging around the third said they had heard about him, but they were vague.

It was mid-spring and a pleasant time for traveling through the countryside. I had not seen the countryside for a long time and it was refreshing and interesting to me. I ventured to suggest this to Cress and she made a sound of derision.

"You ever live in a small town?" she said.

"No."

"Ugh!" she said. "It's like dying."

"That bad?"

"If you don't belong to the 'group', you're nobody; there's nothing to do, nothing to hope for."

"Well, isn't it like that most everywhere? I mean, there's some group you want to belong to—"

"Maybe, but in a small town there's only one group. All or nothing."

So Cress hadn't belonged.

"You were asking about the guitar and how I got started," she said. "You should have seen the mess I got in with that teacher—"

"What was that about?"

"Dirty gossip," she said. "He was a real nice guy—sweet. He was a good teacher, too. He had an orchestra and a band and he gave private lessons, too, and he would sing these songs. I never heard them before.

"So—I was interested and he said if I would get a guitar, he'd give me lessons. I was working at the bakery after school and had some money saved up, so I bought a guitar—just a cheap one. My mother and sister almost killed me! But it was my own money. And the teacher started giving me lessons."

"At home?"

"Yes, because it had to be in the evening because I worked in the afternoons. And pretty soon the gossip got started—people said we were doing what we shouldn't. The teacher almost lost his job over it."

"Was it when that happened you left home?"

"No, not right then. I was only fifteen then."

"Did you graduate from high school?"

"No. I got sick of school."

"When you went to Chicago, what did you hope would happen? What did you have in mind?"

"I don't know—nothing. I just knew I had to have a job and I went to the Mill and Roger gave me a job. It was simple."

"And then you met Richie."

"Yes."

"And all your dreams came true."

"What do you mean by that?"

"I don't know what I mean. Let's have lunch."

In a rustic roadside inn we had lunch and I gave some thought to my map. Roger had mentioned the hootenanny at Champaign, and I had those papers out of Richie's closet, from towns in southeastern Illinois and western Indiana. False or true, they were a kind of lead, and it seemed a waste of time to cover the western part of Illinois. I crossed off everything west of a line through Peoria and Springfield and decided to head more directly toward the crossing into Indiana, by way of Champaign-Urbana.

"You don't remember that Richie ever mentioned this town of Fairmont?" I asked her.

"No," she said. "I guess he probably mentioned it, but I don't remember."

* * * *

It was about an hour later, as we drove southeast on a quiet county road, that I found we were being followed. We were way out in the country now, in farm land, and traffic was sparse and fitful. For several miles we had passed no other car and none had passed us. But there was the one car, steadily behind us, slowing when I slowed, speeding up when I accelerated.

Cress had fallen asleep with her head on my shoulder. After lunch she had been animated for a while, had sung a few songs and then, like a baby, had dropped off. So I was able to give my total, reluctant attention to the threat behind us.

They were driving a large, powerful car and certainly could outrun me in any stretch. That they would try to outrun me, force me off the road and get the thing done quickly, was the most likely of the moves available to them.

They might wait until dark, until we turned in somewhere. But they couldn't foresee what kind of place that would be and whether it would be suitable for their purpose.

Or they might have decided just to tag along until we caught up with Richie. But I thought they cared less about Richie than about that suitcase.

I was left with the probability that they would strike soon, and hard. The attempt, though risky, would not be fantastic. The towns were now ten to twelve miles apart, and in between were farms and wood lots. There would be an occasional tractor crawling bug-like over a fenced field, and occasionally a car or farm truck might pass in one direction or the other. Only by extremely bad luck would they run into interference.

I could see no way to shake them in this environment. I could probably beat them into the next town, where we could hole up for a while. But that would only put off an inevitable encounter later. What I really had to do was to settle them once for all, and the only way to do that was to get them in a bag and ship them to Chicago, where Sergeant Schnell would keep them busy for at least a few days.

A road sign said the next town was five miles straight ahead. I didn't think the ones behind us could manage their coup within that limit and I pushed down on the gas pedal and headed for town. They came along at the customary distance, tried nothing fancy and began to drop back as we entered the outskirts of the village.

It was a single main street with a few stores and service stations on both sides, but it did have a comfortable-looking café on the far side of town, and I pulled up in front of it. Looking back, I saw no sign of the big car, but there were tractors and a few trucks blocking the view. They would be back there somewhere. There was nowhere else to go.

Cress woke up and I gave her time to get the sleep out of her face before we went inside. Leaving the car, I went to the trunk, opened it, taking plenty of time, lifted out the suitcase and carried it in with us.

We were the only customers in the place and the woman who ran the café came from the kitchen to serve us. Cress wanted a glass of orange juice and I ordered pie and coffee. There was a jukebox in the corner and Cress examined the repertoire, put a quarter in the machine and started it going.

I finished my pie and coffee and she was only halfway into her glass of juice. She listened to the music raptly and tapped one foot on the floor.

"Listen," I said, "I've got something has to be done. Will you wait here till I get back? It may be a little while."

"What are you going to do?" she asked.

"Well, I want to ask a few questions around town and get the car checked up—there's a funny rattle in it, I don't know what—and one thing and another. Will you be all right here, listening to the music?"

"I guess so," she said.

I paid our check, picked up the suitcase and started out. She watched me but said nothing.

"Be back pretty soon," I said.

I took the suitcase to the car, locked it in the trunk, got in and pulled away. I turned and went back along the main street and couldn't find any kind of police facility. The town was so small, they would have maybe a night watchman, doubling as sheriff's deputy.

Turning again, I saw the big car parked under a tree about a block away from the café. The two of them were sitting in the front seat, and I passed them slowly enough to make the identification. The one with the low-growing black hair clinched it for me. I was still vague in my memory about the other, but one was enough.

I gathered speed little by little, watching the view in back, and saw them ease out from their tree as I passed the town limits. I made sure they were coming on and not stopping at the café and then began to pay attention to the road again.

The countryside was laid out like a checkerboard, with narrow connecting roads intersecting the county highway at intervals of about half a mile. Between the crossroads were the farms, a cluster of house, barn and outbuildings, set well back among a few trees, the rest of it flat, open fields, with a wood lot in most cases, far off the road. Now and then, where a creek ran close to the highway, there would be foliage and a grove of trees nearby. The road appeared to run straight as an arrow for two miles ahead and then to curve, and in the area of the curve there were trees. If there was a turnoff, it would maybe work out.

I pushed the speed to sixty-five and the big car came on, gradually closing the gap between us. I had no way of knowing that they planned to close in on me so soon, but surely they wouldn't wait indefinitely. There was no profit in chasing me forever down a country road.

I could see now that the curve in the road was very slight, but there were trees and a crossroad cutting into them. The shoulders of the road were high, falling off sharply on both sides, and a concrete culvert marked the turn. It would have to be made slowly and square. If the crossroad ran straight on, I would gain nothing. But if there was a grove there, with access, a private lane…

They were about a hundred and fifty yards behind me as I approached the culvert. I swung wide, hit the brakes and made the sharp, right-angle turn, speeding up as soon as I was straightaway. The crossroad dipped beyond the culvert, crossed a small wooden bridge, then twisted into a grove of trees. There was a cleared space, enough for a car, and tracks leading into it. I angled off the road into the clearing as the big car swung over the culvert, tires screeching. I had my gun out and was leaving the car when they came in sight. They stopped abruptly on the crossroad, skidded a little beyond the back of my car, backed up and stopped again, blocking me from behind. I had moved to the front end of my car where I could watch them along the slope of the hood over the right head lamp.

They came out of the car and they both had guns. It was a bad time.

What were you thinking of? I asked myself. All of a sudden there's more than you can handle and you should have known it. You act like a man trying out for hero of the century.

The one advantage I had was that they had to stay together. If they should spread out, I would get one or the other for sure.

My hat felt too tight for my head and I brushed it off with my arm. One of them took a shot at it as it drifted to the ground. He missed, but not by much.

They were standing close together at the back of my car, trying to find me through the rear window and windshield. I leaned against the head lamp and waited. One of them showed himself at the right rear bumper and I let go at him along the swell of the fender. I was a shade low and the thing ricocheted off the metal and whined into the air beyond him. He ducked out of sight.

"Go ahead, bust the goddam lock," I heard one of them say.

"Bust it with what?" the other said.

"Get something out of the trunk."

"You nuts?"

"All right then, let's rush him."

"Let's think it over," the other said.

It was nice to be in on their planning this way.

"Hey," one of them called. "Hey, you."

I didn't say anything.

"We'll make a deal with you," he said.

"With a gun in your hand?" I said.

"You throw yours out and we'll drop ours."

"Sure you will."

"All we want is that suitcase," he said.

"Why?"

"It belongs to us."

"It's in the trunk," I said, "and the key's in the ignition slot. Come on and get it."

It would have been all right with me. If I could knock out one of them, I could handle the other. It was an odd situation. I could see them behind the car, through that rear window. They could see me, too, if they craned their necks. But they couldn't shoot at me without showing themselves on one side or the other. You shoot through two widely separated thicknesses of safety glass and you can't tell what you'll hit.

"It's worth money to us," one of them called.

"How much?" I said.

I guess they had a conference about it, because there was a period of silence. Then one of them said:

"It depends on when we open the suitcase."

"Oh," I said. "Very sorry."

"You can't stay there forever," he called.

"I can stay here a long, long time."

Another pause. Suddenly the car rocked violently and I banged my head against the rim of the headlamp. They were trying to push it over on me. They found that wouldn't work, and I could see the tops of their heads close together in the middle of the rear window.

I glanced around the clearing and got little comfort out of it. I was standing in deep grass, but not deep enough to hide in. The nearest cover was a clump of trees about twenty feet off my left shoulder, and it wasn't much. Besides, they could pick me off on my way over there. What it began to look like was the stalemate of all time, with none of us able to move from where he was and nothing any of us could do till somebody got careless or impatient.

I thought about that for a while. Sometimes, if they're very neurotic, and they always are, they are also suggestible and jumpy.

I took my fountain pen out of my pocket and balanced it over the gun barrel. I made a coarse hissing sound with my mouth and at the same time, loose-wristed, rattled the pen against the gun. It made a good rattle.

"Oh-oh!" I said. "Watch it, brother."

There was silence.

"That's right, baby," I said, "under the car. Just keep going."

More silence, but only for about thirty seconds. I made the hissing sound again.

"What...?" one of them said.

"Snake," I said. "Rattler. A big one."

One of them mouthed a few bad words.

"It's a con," the other one said. "Shut up."

There was silence for about a minute and a half. Then I heard their feet moving, here and there, not much, just a little. They didn't believe me for a minute, but on the other hand, if it should just happen that there was a rattler under the car—

The sound of their feet stopped and there was some deep silence. I let it have its way with them. The next thing I knew, they were quarreling *sotto voce.*

"—you," one said.

"Somebody's got to—"

"Stick your own goddam face down there."

"I'll match you—"

"Shut up!"

I raised up enough to see them clearly through the car. They had backed off a couple of feet from the bumper and they didn't know what to do. They looked to both sides and then, somewhat longingly, back toward their car. Then they looked at each other. Finally they looked at the ground. They backed off another couple of paces, and I moved out to one side. Just a few more feet back and I could get to them. If I could get them in the legs, I thought, it would soften them up enough. I had manacles in the trunk. If I could get them into the car, I could drive them to the nearest sheriff's station and unload them. But they would have to back off a little more.

One of them was studying the ground hard.

"There he is!" he said.

"Hold it!" the other said. "I don't see nothing."

"Right over there, under the taillight."

"It's a goddam rock."

Off to my right there was a remote rumble, growing steadily in volume. A tractor, coming down the crossroad, I decided.

No good, I thought. Somebody'll get hurt for sure and we'll have a mess.

"Well, then what—" one of them said.

"Not me," the other said. "I'm not going near that car."

"Then let's rush him, get it over with."

"Rush the snake, you stupid—?"

"All right then, let's go."

We moved simultaneously as they broke for their car. It was a short distance, and I was out far enough to draw a good bead, but just as I caught my breath to squeeze off, this damn tractor came tumbling into sight, out of control, plowing off the road toward the clearing. Nobody driving it.

I heard their car doors slam and the motor roar. A few seconds later it backed, lurching, toward the highway, out of sight. The tractor came on like a monster, glanced off a tree, swerved, banged into another tree and came to a stop about three feet from the rear fender of my car.

I put my gun away, picked up my hat, straightened it out and put it on. I dusted my pants and straightened my necktie and said a few things of no great importance and walked out to the crossroad. A man in overalls, dusting a straw hat against his pants legs, came limping toward the clearing. He was not in good spirits.

"What the hell is going on here?" he said.

He set his hat on his head and pulled it down tight across his brown, lined face. He was chewing tobacco and he let go a long streamer of brown juice that missed my shoes by about two inches.

"Those two," I said, "wanted. I almost had 'em."

"Wanted for what?" he said.

"Murder," I said.

He wasn't interested. He looked at his tractor up against the tree, took out a big red handkerchief and blew his nose and stuffed the handkerchief back in his pants.

"Crazy goddam fools," he muttered, "wavin' them guns around—damn near broke my hip, leavin' the machine. Goddam it—"

"I'm sorry," I said.

"Who are you?" he said.

"I'm a cop," I said.

"Where from?"

"Chicago," I said.

"Oh," he said, and turned his back on me.

He walked over to the tractor and stood looking at it and I knew the interview was over. I got in my car, managed to back it into the crossroad without knocking anything over and got out on the highway. The big car was out of sight.

So we get to do it all over again, somewhere, sometime, I thought.

I started back toward town, not pushing it.

CHAPTER NINE

In a service-station washroom I cleaned myself up while they took care of the car. When I got to the café Cress and the proprietress, a large woman with fluffy gray hair and a well-creased face, were sitting at the table with their heads together over a piece of paper. Cress was doing the writing. The woman started to get up when I came in, but Cress put out a hand.

"Wait a minute," she said, "I don't have that last line yet."

"Well, I have to get back to my chores—"

"Just do it once more, the last three lines."

With a shy glance at me the woman sang, in a light, breathy voice. I couldn't make it out and waited near the counter, while she sang and Cress wrote busily.

"Now," she said, "let's see if I got the whole thing."

She sang, reading from the paper, a mournful, dirge-like song about a girl who dreamed all her life about owning a rare white horse and finally she got the horse and the horse threw her and killed her.

"Yes," the woman said, "that's the way I remember it. Don't know what you want with an old song like that."

"It's beautiful!" Cress said.

The woman laughed and headed for the kitchen. Cress was on her feet, waving the paper. She kissed it and held out her arms wide, ecstatically.

"My own song!" she said. "It's one her grandmother used to sing to her…"

"That's fine," I said.

She stopped in the middle of the room and sang it again, while the woman looked out over the service bar from the kitchen. When she finished, we both applauded.

"Guess what?" Cress said.

"What?"

"There's going to be a hoot tomorrow at—" She called toward the kitchen, "What was the name of that town?"

The woman mentioned a college town farther south.

"Over by Danville," she said.

"And guess what again?" Cress said. "Reuben will be there."

"Well," I said, "then we'd better get started."

"All right. Thanks for the song!" Cress called.

The woman laughed heartily.

"Sure, honey. Let me know when it goes on the radio."

Cress ran ahead of me to the car, waving the paper in the air.

"Need my guitar," she said.

I got it out of the trunk and she climbed into the back seat with it. We started down the highway and she was at work, looking for the music on the strings and singing the sad song under her breath.

I kept looking for the big car with the two slugs in it, but there was a truckload of hay behind us and I couldn't see what was behind that, and we led that load of hay all the way to the county seat, where I pulled up at the sheriff's office.

"What for?" Cress said vaguely.

"Want to check on something," I said. "You like to come along?"

"No, I'm busy," she said.

I left her with her song and went into the station. It took me a few minutes to get onto a responsible officer, a middle-aged man with deep pouches under his eyes and gnarled, arthritic hands. He sat hunched over a minute, cluttered desk in a small room with three other desks crowding it, one of which was in use.

I described the big car, gave him the license number and descriptions of the occupants and told him they were wanted in Chicago and although I couldn't put a finger on them right at the moment, they were certainly in the vicinity.

"What are they wanted for?" he asked.

"Assault. You can check with Sergeant Schnell in the robbery division."

"Sergeant Schnell," he said, writing.

I got up to leave and he said:

"Wait a minute. Sergeant Schnell?"

"Yeah."

He was pawing through an accumulation of papers, wanted posters and bulletins. He came up with a teletype communication, blue ink on yellowish paper, and read it. His lips moved soundlessly.

"Richie Darden," he said, "a folk singer. Is he one of 'em?"

"No," I said. "No, this is two other guys."

"Oh," he said. "Sergeant Schnell is pretty busy, isn't he?"

"You know how it goes."

"Yes, sir, I know how it goes. Thanks for dropping in. I'll put out a thing on it."

"I'll be pulling out of town right away," I said, "and they'll probably follow me."

"Well, where's your car?"

I told him.

"I'll see if we got anybody can tag along for a while."

He got on the phone and said something with reference to my license number, then nodded goodbye and went on to other things. I went back to the car and pulled away slowly. A sheriff's car pulled out behind me and it followed me for several miles, but it was the only car that did and finally it turned off on a side road. By then it was late afternoon, we were on a state highway, heading for Danville, and the traffic was heavy. I couldn't see whether the big car was back there or not.

So Schnell did it, I thought. He put out a thing for Richie Darden.

All I heard from Cress was the song about the little girl and the white horse, all the way to Danville.

* * * *

Approaching Danville, I came to a complex of bypass turnoffs, with a good many signs, and pulled off to study my road map. The college town toward which we were headed was off to the south and west. Cress had fallen silent and I assumed she was asleep, but then I heard her say quietly:

"If we don't turn off here, we'll have to go all the way through Danville and it takes more time."

I put the map away and got started.

"You know this country pretty well," I said.

"I was born around here."

"Not in Danville?"

"No, a little town down the road."

I didn't press it and she didn't volunteer any more on it. She was sitting up with her guitar across her knees, but looking out now, not singing. I recalled there had been two small towns on the road to our destination. The first one we reached was called Hilldale and it was little more than a milk stop: a couple of stores, a service station and a railroad freight depot. Seven miles farther on we came to a larger town named Carrollton. It had a population of two thousand plus, a wide tree-lined main street with big houses on broad lawns, a lighted business district that stretched out for three or four blocks, with a couple of secondary business streets intersecting it, and a small factory at the far end, built on the bank of a river. As we drove through it, I watched Cress. She sat quietly, looking out, her face impassive. In the center of town we had to stop for a traffic signal and she hunched down in her seat, as if to make herself invisible. After that she appeared to take no more interest in the town.

I said nothing until we were some miles beyond it.

"Cress," I said, "what's your last name? How does it happen I never asked your last name?"

"I don't know. Why?"

"Just curious."

It was a long time coming. But she told me, quietly, and I heard her fingers brush across the strings of her guitar.

"Fanio," she said. "Crescentia Fanio is my name."

A faint shiver went down my back. It seemed, as a moment of disclosure, over-portentous.

Why? I wondered.

Because maybe it's like this—now she has a song, she can have a name.

Crescentia Fanio, I thought. A nice name. And the other kids would pronounce it "Fanny-oh," as a rib; just a harmless childish joke.

We came into the college town, somewhat larger than Carrollton, but not much different, except for the campus on the near edge of town, a collection of old and new buildings set on rolling hills, with a good many trees around the older ones and not much landscaping for the newer.

The only commercial accommodations in the middle of town were housed in a crumbling hotel. I drove on through and there were two or three motels on the outskirts, but no vacancies in any of them. There had been a good many signs in town about the hootenanny coming up the next day, and I decided everyone had got there ahead of us.

"I guess it's back to Danville for the night," I said.

"All right," Cress said. "They'll have some coffeehouses in Danville."

During the return trip she sang fitfully, except that she was silent as we drove through Carrollton. When we had passed through it and were out on the highway again, she resumed singing.

I found a hotel with a garage and we checked in there. It felt more secure than a motel on the edge of the city. Cress stayed with the car in the garage while I checked us in and we took everything up to the suite, including those papers from Richie Darden's closet, Cress's guitar and her new song.

"We'll freshen up and have a good dinner, all right?" I said.

"All right," she said. I started into my own room and she said, "Listen, Richie was in Danville, quite a lot. I remember. He sang a song about Danville, too."

"Well, we'll ask around town," I said.

She began humming a tune under her breath. I closed the door, got undressed and into the bathtub. Lying there, soaking out the frustrations of the day, I could hear the plaintive wailing of her song like a lamentation from long ago. It was getting under my skin.

* * * *

During my leisurely preparations for setting out once more she cooked up a surprise for me. When I finally knocked at the connecting door, she sang out:

"Wait a minute!"

"No hurry," I said.

After about fifteen minutes she said, "All right—now!"

I opened the door and she was dressed. Not only was she dressed, she was dressed up. No pedal pushers, sandals and sweater tonight. She was wearing a cocktail dress, stockings and real shoes, and she had spent a long time brushing and pinning up her hair, very high over her long face. Despite her limitations—her small, almost spindly shape and the incongruously golden hair over the dark eyes and brows—she had achieved a stunning effect.

"Hey, you're beautiful," I said.

"Do I look all right?"

"I can't say—I don't have any breath."

She smiled.

"You're just saying that," she said.

"I'll prove it with champagne."

I reached for the telephone and she laughed and held my wrist.

"No," she said. "Don't waste champagne on me. I hate it."

She was shy again and wouldn't look at me.

"I just thought maybe I would see if I could look like not a tramp," she said.

"You look like not a tramp the best I ever saw," I said.

"Then I can go to dinner with you?"

"Try standing me up and see what happens," I said.

I offered my arm with overzealous gallantry and she accepted with exaggerated graciousness. We got to the door, stopped and looked back at Richie Darden's suitcase, on the floor near the bed. We looked at each other.

"It'll be all right if we lock the door," she said.

But she was trying too hard.

"We'll just take it down and check it at the desk," I said. "Then we won't have to worry about it."

She waited while I got it and we went out to the hall. As I closed the door, she leaned close and kissed me on the cheek.

"Thanks, Mac," she said.

"Don't mention it. I'd climb the highest mountain."

She squeezed my arm with those sharp nails.

"You're crazy," she said.

We had dinner in the hotel dining room, and she ate well and with first-class manners. I was proud of her.

"Because you've been so good," I said, "I'll take you to one of them underground places, one of them coffeehouses."

"I'm too young," she said.

"Never too young."

She looked at me across the rim of her coffee cup.

"Crescentia," I said. "Crescentia Fanio."

She tilted the cup slowly, hiding her eyes.

We left the hotel, found a taxi and started the rounds of the coffee-houses—the few there were—and we ran into a thing. A fancy name for what we ran into would be "wall of silence."

At the first place we stopped business was quite good, probably because of the combination of the hoot the next day and the fact that it was Friday night. We sat through some songs by a trio of girls and a soloist named Joe Finney. They were a disappointment to both of us and we prowled around till we found the manager in the foyer, with three of the faithful gathered around. When a break came, I edged in and asked if anyone had heard from Richie Darden lately. One of the guys in the cluster had a guitar. He twanged a deep-toned string, looked at the manager and looked away. The manager looked at me and at Cress and the others looked at us and they all turned away, and the manager said:

"No—nothing."

Then he turned away. Cress and I looked at their backs and then at each other and left the place.

In the next two hours we went to three other coffeehouses and the same thing happened with minor variations. By then it was midnight. Cress's spirits had dropped along with some strands of her carefully arranged hair. She walked as if her feet hurt. In silence we climbed into the last taxi and went back to the hotel.

Cress sat on the edge of her bed and kicked off her shoes. Her arms rose wearily and she took the pins out of her hair. It fell around her shoulders and across her face.

"What happened?" she said. "Why won't anybody talk about Richie?"

"I don't know," I said.

But I thought I knew all right. Sergeant Schnell had sent out his little message. The word was out for Richie Darden. This kind of word spreads fast. The band had closed ranks. From now on information about Richie Darden would be hard to come by among his own kind.

"At the hoot tomorrow," she said, "somebody will know. Reuben will know about Richie."

"Reuben will know?" I said.

"Sure. Richie and Reuben were friends. They worked some of the same places. Reuben will know."

"I hope so," I said.

She lay back on the bed with her arms over her face. I made sure her door was locked and turned down the lights.

"I'm sorry," she said, in a muffled tone. "I wasn't much of a date."

I leaned over and kissed her.

"You're a real good date," I said. "If I play my cards right, maybe you'll let me take you to the hoot tomorrow."

She put her hand on my face, patting.

"Any time," she said.

I went to my own room and got into bed and eventually I fell asleep. I don't know how long Cress lay awake, but she slept in very late in the morning. I woke around eight o'clock and ordered up some breakfast. While I waited for it, I sorted out those newspapers I'd picked up from the apartment they had shared and put them in chronological order. There were four from a town in Illinois called Bruno, three from Fallon, Indiana, and half a dozen from Fairmont, Indiana. They were all weeklies and the oldest date on any of them was about ten weeks previous. The latest was a month old.

I checked my road map and found Fairmont to be the farthest east of any of the towns and not too far from Danville. It was located on the Wabash River, was the county seat of a rural county, with a population of over ten thousand. The town of Fallon was back up the road from Fairmont about ten miles. It was a very small country town, also on the river. Bruno, Illinois, was between Danville and Fallon.

With this geographical background established, I started through the papers. In the Bruno papers there was absolutely nothing that caught my eye. A typical farming community, it produced the local news you would expect to find, and none of it had significance for me.

To read every word of a newspaper in a search for a name is a rough job. I drank four cups of coffee and it got me through Bruno and halfway through Fallon. I switched then to the Fairmont papers, which were somewhat more interesting, but also much thicker. There was nothing about Richie Darden anywhere. The most exciting thing that had happened in Fairmont for a long time, I gathered, was the great payroll robbery at some local factory, and this had happened five months before. The only news on it was that there was no news of the robbers after all that time.

I heard Cress stirring around and gave up on the papers for the time being. Whatever Richie Darden had wanted from them had eluded me.

I had them neatly stacked up and was lifting the Fallon papers onto the others when an item caught my eye, a front-page story that I should have caught right away.

"Army Sergeant Returns to Family Home," the headline read. The story said simply: "Master Sergeant Clare Duffy, USA Retired, is returning to take up residence in the old family home near Fallon. Old-timers will remember the Duffy farm, two miles west of town on the riverbank, where four generations of Sergeant Duffy's family have lived and worked. The site was homesteaded by Albert Duffy in 1853. Sergeant Duffy has retired from a distinguished career in the United States Army and his many friends will welcome him home."

I read it twice, got out my map and made a circle approximately two miles west of Fallon. And about then Cress knocked at the door.

I opened it to find her swathed in that bathrobe, rubbing her eyes and smiling shyly under her hands.

"Is this the train to Hootenanny Holler?" she said.

"Well," I said, "if it ain't, I'm a dad-busted dingbat."

She looked up with her dark eyes and rubbed her hand across her nose.

"Hey, Daddy," she said, "when you get with it, you go all the way, huh?"

"What do you want for breakfast?"

"Whatever you had."

I picked up the telephone as she turned away. I decided the news about Clare Duffy returning to the old homestead could wait till after the hoot.

CHAPTER TEN

The hootenanny convened in the football stadium and the turnout, though not to be compared with a football crowd, must have been gratifying to the sponsors. By the time we got there, shortly after noon, only the higher seats and those at the far end were empty. A stage had been set up at one end of the field and there were rows of folding chairs for those who intended to participate. We didn't know about this till we got to the gate, and Cress drew me aside.

"We have to get somewhere close to Reuben," she said. "How can we talk to him from way up there?"

"Well," I said, "why not participate?"

"What?"

"You have a song—sing it."

"In front of all these people? Listen—"

"You'll knock the spots off everybody here. Have to start some time. Why not now?"

"No, Mac—I couldn't."

"Come on, let's get the guitar. You can think it over on the way."

We walked back to the car, which took ten minutes, got the guitar out, and she found the paper on which she had written the words of the song. Her fingers were shaking as she folded and tucked it into the bodice of the gingham dress she was wearing. It was a pink dress, and she was wearing white socks and shoes. She looked like a walking testimonial for the Four-H clubs.

While she gathered her song and guitar together, I took the occasion to rubberneck around the shaded street where we had parked, along with several hundred others. There was no sign of the two guys I had played duck-the-snake with the day before. We had not checked out of the hotel and we had left the precious suitcase at the desk, so we had little to lose by them, except that if they were still onto us, they might do some damage to the car. I didn't know whether they were onto us or not, but I hadn't done much to shake them off.

I carried the guitar to the stadium and handed it to her as we reached the gate. One of the boys manning the entrance pointed to a box on a stand.

"Take a number," he said.

"A number?"

"Yeah. That's your number—tells when you'll go on. Give your name to the man over there at the table."

"Oh," she said, and took a number.

We went inside and a couple of men in shirt sleeves sat at a long table with clipboards and pencils.

"Number forty-eight," one of them said, when Cress handed over her tab.

The other fellow asked for her name. She looked at me.

"Cress," she said.

"Cress what?"

"Cress—Darden."

"Do you sing?"

"Uh—yes, sir."

"What's the name of your song?"

"Uh…" She pulled the paper out of her bodice and flipped it open. "The White Horse Song," she said.

"The White Horse Song," he repeated, and wrote it down. "All right, Cress. Just a minute—this gentleman—"

He had me dead to rights. I couldn't leave her alone in that milling throng, and I was damned if I would get up there and sing a song, even if I had to.

"We're together," I said.

"You sing together?" he said doubtfully.

"No—"

"I'm sorry, but only the performers are allowed on the field."

Cress leaned across the table, her small breasts rising and falling with agitation, her face pink.

"Listen, mister," she said, "this is my father. I got a kind of a thing about crowds. I'd be deathly afraid to stay here all by myself."

He looked at her and then he looked at me and at his partner and finally he shrugged and said:

"All right, go ahead."

"Come on, Daddy," Cress said.

We left the table and wandered over to the folding chairs lined up in rows facing the stage. There were about a hundred and fifty chairs, most of them occupied. There were a great many guitars, some violins and a few banjos. The people in the chairs ranged in age from about six to seventy-five, and everybody was getting along just fine with everybody else. A quartet of boys in western clothes was practicing in a tight huddle off to one side. Others were tuning or strumming guitars in solitary concentration. A girl of ten or twelve stood with stretched throat, her face lifted, warbling like a canary into the air.

We found two chairs at the end of the fourth row and Cress laid her guitar case across them.

"That's us," she said.

"You and your daddy," I said.

She blushed.

"I had to think of something," she said.

"You did all right. I couldn't think of a thing."

We asked an elderly woman with hair like pink champagne when the proceedings were scheduled to begin, and she said at two o'clock. She had a box lunch on the ground under her chair. It smelled like fried chicken and I salivated richly.

"How about a hot dog?" I said.

"Sure," Cress said.

Some stands had been set up around the edges of the stadium to purvey sandwiches, soft drinks and coffee. We stood in line at one of them for about twenty minutes, and when we finally made it, they had run out of everything except chicken salad sandwiches and orange pop. We moved to the next and stood in that line. It worked out all right; we got two hot dogs each and two cups of coffee.

We leaned against the wall surrounding the stadium field and went after our hot dogs.

"I'm so scared I'm out of my mind," she said.

"You're bound to be scared. Just don't panic."

"I might. What if I get up there and start screaming for Daddy?"

"I'll come up and get you."

"I bet that's a song they never heard before."

"You have a good song and you know how to sing it," I said. "Don't worry."

"Hah," she said. "Don't worry, he says."

A young couple in matching blue jeans and sweaters stood not far off along the wall.

"He is not!" the girl said. "Reuben is the greatest, the absolutely most."

"Reuben," the boy said tauntingly. "All you can think is Reuben. 'Reuben, Reuben, I been thinkin'—'"

The girl put her hand over his mouth.

"Shut up," she said.

"This Reuben is pretty great, huh?" I said.

"He's good," Cress said. "Mighty good."

"What it looks like to me," I said, "it looks like a bunch of hillbillies off the reservation for the first time."

"Well," she said, "it's different from Chicago or Los Angeles or New York. I mean it's different from a coffeehouse. This is just a bunch of people get together to sing songs. Anything wrong with that?"

"Nothing," I said. "And Reuben is kind of the special attraction?"

"That's right."

"Would they come like this to listen to each other, if Reuben wasn't going to be here?"

"They might. Not so many though."

"I'm glad they turned out good for Reuben."

"Daddy," she said, "buy me another hot dog."

We went back and stood in line some more and got another hot dog and some coffee. There were sounds of music, fragmentary and cacophonous, from all sides. A group in the stands had started singing cowboy songs. We stood below, chewing our hot dogs, listening.

"I can't do it," Cress said.

"Can't do what?"

"Get up there and sing."

"Yes, you can. But don't have a nervous breakdown. We'll find another way to get to Reuben."

"I don't know if we can. He'll be surrounded all the time."

"We'll do our best."

We finished our coffee and wandered back to our seats. The elderly lady was eating from her box lunch.

"May I get you a cup of coffee, ma'am?" I said.

"Say now, that would be nice," she said. "Here, I've got some money in my purse…"

"Please let me do it," I said. "I feel very big today."

She smiled in a friendly way and I went to stand in line for some coffee. When I returned with it, Cress had her guitar out of her case and was standing with one foot on her chair, the guitar across her thigh, tuning it. I handed the cup of coffee to the lady, who accepted with thanks and promptly burned her tongue.

"Is Reuben here yet?" Cress said.

"I wouldn't know," I said. "Do you know, ma'am?"

The lady looked surprised.

"Heavens!" she said. "Who is Reuben?"

Cress looked at me blankly and strummed her guitar.

Two men were on the stage, adjusting the mike and fiddling with the sound system. They produced a variety of noises, some of which echoed piercingly over the stadium and caused the crowd to shriek in protest, finally satisfied themselves and came down from the platform. The lines at the refreshment stands were thinning out, and most of the performers' seats were filled now. The huddling quartet had stopped practicing and the little girl with the sweet throat was sitting with her hands in her lap, looking straight ahead.

Someone spoke hoarsely behind us:

"There he is!"

A small group stood on the grass near the stage. One of them had a guitar slung from his shoulder, so casually it seemed a part of his clothing, as if he wore it day and night and would be naked without it. He stood well over six feet four, and he was rangy, with long arms and legs. He wore jeans and a sweater and his hair was long and combed straight back from his face, which was lean and square-jawed, with a prominent nose. There was a strangeness about him neither sinister nor theatrical. He was a man to look at with wonder, and I was curious about the sound he would make.

"That's Reuben?" Cress said.

"I guess so," I said.

"Who is Reuben?" the old lady said.

It was hot, sitting in the sun. I couldn't take my coat off because I had the gun on. It was irritating to feel the need of it and frustrating that I had no way to shed it. Cress had her guitar to fool around with and keep herself occupied. All I could do was to sit and steam and wish they would get their show on the road.

They got it going in fairly good time, but it was a long wait from where I sat. Without any warning, "The Star-Spangled Banner" blasted out of the loudspeakers and everybody stood up and sang, and we all sat down again and by then Reuben and three other men had mounted the stage and were sitting up there, and one of the men got up and opened the program. He was mercifully brief and put Reuben on right away.

Reuben came on singing. He walked to the mike, struck a chord and sang a short railroad ballad, a variation on the "dying engineer" theme. He had a deep, resonant voice and he projected with vigor, but even to my ear it was obviously not a sophisticated, trained voice. He used what he had and sang from his guts.

The applause was loud and sustained and all he did by way of acknowledgment was to raise his hand for quiet. He sang an old stand-by, a version of the "Oh, who will shoe your feet?" song. And then he sang a rollicking nonsense song, inviting the audience to join in the refrain. He kept it up till they were going good and strong and then he got into the hootenanny.

"Plenty of folks here today," he said, "and plenty of songs to be sung. Let's sing 'em! Bring on the 'Wabash Minstrels'!"

A trio of teen-age boys with guitars ran on stage and went right to it with a number called "Roll, River, Roll." They went over very big and Reuben brought them back for an encore. They were followed by a man-and-wife team. The man played the fiddle and the woman sang a dance tune that sounded like "Skip to My Lou" and filled in with some fancy footwork. They, too, were heartily received. There followed a little guy about seven years old, dressed in a cowboy outfit. He played a ukulele and sang a western song. Halfway along in it he forgot the words. He stood there in helpless bewilderment for about five seconds, then Reuben came out and squatted down beside him and they finished it together.

And so it went. They took a break roughly every half hour, and every once in a while Reuben would sing a solo number, then bring on the next group. The big break came at three-thirty, and they had worked down through number thirty-nine, which meant that Cress would be coming up soon.

We went for refreshments during the break and got into the shade of the grandstand.

"Feel my hands," Cress said. "Like ice. I can't play the guitar—I'll freeze!"

"Reuben will warm you up," I said.

She wasn't listening. She stood with her head back and her eyes closed, her mouth making the words of her song. I caught sight of Reuben with a couple of young men near one of the hot-dog stands.

"Maybe we could catch him right now," I said. "He's right over there."

We started in his direction, but the group drifted off toward the stage and we couldn't catch up with him without making a nuisance out of it. We went back to our seats and the old lady had left. It turned out she was the next one on. She sang unaccompanied, a long, dirge-like ballad. It was interminable, and her voice had absolutely no color. Cress began to groan and the crowd got very restless around us. It would have been a fiasco under other conditions, but everyone was in this together and nobody could hold it against her.

Cress's countdown began—forty-one, forty-two, forty-three. At forty-four she had her fingers in her mouth. I put my arm around her and she leaned against me, shaking.

"Just make believe you're, all alone, singing to Richie," I said.

"I never sing to Richie," she moaned.

"Then sing it to me. Just to me," I said.

On stage Reuben was calling number forty-seven.

"Come on now," I said, "big girl. Pick up your guitar and walk right up there."

She got on her feet as if sleepwalking. I handed her the guitar and she walked away toward the stage. She looked impossibly tiny and fragile in the sunlight, making the long, hard walk.

"Next," Reuben said to the mike, "Miss Cress Darden…" He paused. Then he repeated it. "Cress Darden, singing 'The White Horse Song.'"

I watched her cross the stage. Reuben waited for her at the mike, leaned down and spoke to her. She said something, brushed at her face, and Reuben gave her a pat on the shoulder. She was on.

At first it was hard to catch her words. She was badly frightened and the guitar covered her voice. But after a few bars, she firmed up, her tone deepened and she sang it out in good style.

The people listened. I noticed Reuben listening, his head turned, his eyes on her. It was a good, original song and it seemed appropriate to her: the little girl with the dream of a great white horse, the long years of waiting, the dream come true:

> *Now her own white horse with snowy mane*
> *She could ride to her heart's content.*

And the ending, dolorous, tragic:

> *They mercifully killed the great white horse,*
> *To ease its misery and pain;*
> *And she lies at peace 'neath the willow tree,*
> *Never to ride again.*

There was a silence when she finished, then applause, generous and prolonged. She started off and Reuben caught her arm. They stood for some time, while Cress shook her head stubbornly, and I gathered he was trying to get her to do another. But he gave up finally and let her go.

There was applause in our own vicinity as she reached her seat and sank into it, panting.

"Oh God," she murmured. "Never again…"

I took her hand and eased the guitar out of it. Her hand was wet and her hair clung damply to her neck.

"You were terrific," I said.

"He kept asking me to sing another one and I wouldn't—I think he's mad at me."

"No, he isn't. Just relax now. Didn't you hear the applause?"

"No. I couldn't hear anything. I could hardly hear him talking to me."

"You were great. Believe me."

A face leaned over between us.

"Where did you get that song?" a woman asked.

"Somebody sang it for me," Cress said. "Up the road—I forget where."

"Wonderful song," the woman said. "You were lovely."

"Thanks," Cress said. "Say—where's the little girl's room?"

"Over there," the woman said. "You go in the west tunnel and turn right. You'll find it."

Cress got up and started away. I gave it a moment's thought and went after her. It was after four o'clock now and the sun was low and red over the rim of the stadium. I couldn't see her clearly, walking away over the grass. I kept thinking, if something should happen to her—if she shouldn't come back—I don't know what I'd do.

Blinking in the sudden dimness under the stadium, I found her walking down an aisle toward the rest rooms. I leaned against one of the girders that supported the stands to wait for her. Echoing hollowly in the steel and concrete framework, I could hear the songs from the stage, all manner of songs in all kinds of voices, high, low and in-between. I looked out at the field just as the sun dropped below the high west wall of the stadium, and the sudden shadow fell like a cold blanket.

Shortly there was a pause in the sound and then Reuben's voice in a few words to close the hoot. But they wouldn't let him off so easy. Applause rose like a storm, faded, and he sang "Barbara Allen," which only raised a greater storm.

"Let's all sing 'The Ash Grove.'"

He started it for them, and little by little various sections of the audience joined in till they were all singing the mournful classic.

Cress came back, looking better than she had looked after her stint.

"We'd better get out there and try to nail him," I said. "I think they're about to fold up."

"Listen," she said. "When he announced me—Cress Darden, remember? He stopped and looked at me. Then he announced it."

"I remember."

"And after, when he was trying to get me to do another, he said, 'Your name is Darden?' And I said yes, because what else could I say, and he didn't say anything. That's when he stopped asking me."

"We'll go have a talk with him."

"Mac—I'm afraid—"

"Nothing to be afraid of," I said.

We walked out of the tunnel and across the shadowed grass to our chairs, and she put the guitar in the case and handed it to me.

They had finished "The Ash Grove," and the people were making their way out of the stands. In the performer's section there was the soft clatter of instruments being gathered up, the muffled tramping of feet.

There was quite a large group on the stage, surrounding Reuben, and it broke up more slowly.

"He's mad at me," Cress said. "Because I wouldn't sing another song. But I couldn't—"

"Now stop it," I said. "It's up to you to say whether you want to sing or not. He knows that as well as anybody."

"I'm so hungry," she said. "I'm starving."

"We'll go have a good dinner somewhere."

One by one the people came down from the stage. Reuben was left with one talkative hanger-on, from whom he was trying to get separated. They drifted toward the steps and came down slowly, a middle-aged guy with a sheaf of papers in one hand, yakking into Reuben's ear. At the bottom of the steps Reuben caught sight of Cress. He shook hands with the man and said:

"Very nice meeting you. Got to rest up now, for tonight."

"Yes, sure," the man said. "See you later. We certainly do appreciate—"

"Yes," Reuben said. "Excuse me."

He left the man standing with his papers and came over to us.

"Hello," he said. "You're the girl sang 'The White Horse Song.'"

"Yes, sir," Cress said.

"That's a good song. I'd like to learn that song."

She pulled the paper out of her bosom and thrust it at him.

"Here it is," she said. "I wrote down the words."

"Well, you can't just hand it over like that," he said.

"Sure. Go ahead," she said.

"Well, I'll get in touch with you about it. You're coming over to the Caboose tonight, aren't you?"

"The Caboose?" she said.

"The coffeehouse here. Going to sing some songs there tonight, for the college folks."

"Oh, sure," she said.

He glanced at me.

"Very fine program," I said. "Been wanting a chance to tell you."

"Thank you," he said.

"Understand you're acquainted with Richie Darden," I said.

He looked at Cress and at me again.

"Yes," he said, "I've met Richie Darden. He has some good songs—good guitar man."

He looked at Cress.

"Your name is Darden. Are you related to Richie?"

"No—not exactly," she said.

"His name is made up," Reuben said. "Made me wonder when you mentioned your name. Kind of a coincidence."

"I guess so," she said. "But I knew Richie."

"Do you have any idea how we could get in touch with him?" I asked. "We've been trying to reach him."

He looked at me for some time. He had a steady, probing gaze. I almost shifted my feet but caught myself in time. His eyes were saying, "Who are you, mister?"

"No," he said finally. "I haven't heard of Richie for some time now."

"I heard he was traveling down this way," I said. "Illinois and Indiana. You might have run into him."

He looked at me some more and his eyes had closed up against me.

"No," he said firmly. "Can't help you."

Someone came toward us.

"Got to go now," he said. "You come around to the Caboose tonight and we'll talk about that song."

"All right," Cress said.

He went off with the guy who had approached us and we stood in the deserted stadium till he disappeared.

"Still hungry?" I asked.

"I don't know," she said. "I guess so."

We started away toward the entrance.

"The Caboose?" I said.

"Danville is kind of a railroad town," she said. "Richie sang a railroad song about Danville."

CHAPTER ELEVEN

The caboose was sumptuous by coffeehouse standards. A long, carpeted room, it featured a fireplace with a raised hearth and a U-shaped cluster of sofas drawn up to it. Chairs were scattered here and there, with tables or stands within reach. When Cress and I arrived, all the chairs were filled and even the floor was crowded with sitting and standing guests. In fact, there was a momentary hitch over our admission. The husky kid in blue jeans who confronted us at the door apologized that the house was full.

"Reuben asked us to come," I said.

He looked doubtful.

"'The White Horse Song'?" Cress said.

"Oh," he said. "Yeah, come in."

We picked our way to a corner where there was room for the two of us to sit on a couple of cushions with our backs to the wall.

Cress was conspicuous in her pink gingham dress. It was a college crowd and the standard costume was slacks, jeans, or leotards, with sweaters or jackets. The long hair fit in just right, though.

The minimum tab for the evening was two dollars a person, and a girl, distinguishable from the others by the fact that she wore an apron like a white leaf over her black leotard, brought us rich black coffee with whipped cream on it. Beer and wine were also available.

Reuben was not yet in evidence, but surrounding comment indicated he would appear any minute. Somehow—I forget the specific context—Cress emitted the name Richie Darden. A girl in front of us turned and said:

"Did you say Richie Darden? He was *here!* Couple of weeks ago—"

The muscular arm of her companion encircled her neck and most of her face.

"Come on, shut up," he said.

Cress looked at me and I looked away from the question in her eyes. Reuben's entrance covered me with some justification.

A cleared space had been left in the center of the room and in it he paced about and sang his songs. Beyond an occasional introductory comment, he spoke very little. His communication was by song and he limited himself to it. In the close, intimate surroundings without any intervening sound system, I could hear how good he was at his trade. His voice, basically deep and rugged, was flexible, and he could adapt it to the feeling of each song. He had a good falsetto and slid in and out of it with ease. His long face had a brooding quality that in no way detracted from the mood he tried to establish.

Apparently he knew every song ever sung and plenty that these people never heard. Also, he was generous. He sang a set of his own choosing, drank a cup of coffee and sang a set of requests. He had been on for almost an hour when he caught sight of Cress in the corner. I noticed the moment of recognition, but beyond that his face said nothing and I couldn't tell whether he was pleased or even interested. He finished the set, had another cup of coffee, and the break went on for some time, as he fell into this or that conversation—mostly as a listener.

He returned again, sang a short, macabre song he claimed to have learned from a Negro en route to his own lynching. Then, without any advance notice, he announced Cress's presence.

"Young lady here tonight," he said, "with a good song. We heard it this afternoon, and maybe if we treat her nice, she'll let us hear it again."

Cress made a whimpering sound in her throat and pressed into me as if she would crawl into my pocket.

"Come on—chin up," I said.

They were clapping in rhythmic demand and Reuben leaned toward Cress with his hand outstretched. Cress raised her empty hands.

"No guitar—" she said.

"Use mine," he said.

"I—couldn't. It's too big."

"I'll get it from the car," I said.

"You traitor," she mumbled.

I made my way to the door and outside. The fresh air felt good and I didn't hurry. Such parking space as they had near the place had been filled when we arrived and we had left the car on the street, a country road some distance from town and the campus. It was dark, the shoulder of the road was rough and I stumbled twice on my way.

I took time to get out the flashlight and check over the car. There was no evidence that it had been tampered with. A few other cars were scattered here and there, most of them on the other side, and none was familiar to me. I replaced the flashlight, got hold of the guitar case and went back inside.

Reuben had got Cress away from the wall and was talking to her at one side of the small space in the center. He had to stoop to reach her level and he looked ungainly, deformed, with his long legs twisted and the guitar flung out on his hip.

I took the guitar out of the case for her and she began to tune it. Her face was flushed, her hands shaky, but she wasn't backing down. I stepped over some people, got back in the corner, and Reuben put her on with simplicity:

"Cress Darden," he said, "'The White Horse Song'—a good song."

The audience fell respectfully silent. Stretching his long legs, Reuben climbed over the people and stood against the wall beside me while she sang.

I don't know whether she had picked up confidence after the cold plunge of the afternoon, or whether something in the mood Reuben had already built up sustained her, but she was good—mighty good. When she finished, they gave her the same tribute of momentary silence, then rousing applause. Reuben did nothing to cut in on it. He stayed where he was, his long face tilted, head back against the wall, and as the applause began to fade I heard him talking to me.

"What is she to you, mister?" he said.

"I'm on hire to her. Richie Darden was her white horse. She lost him, and we're looking."

"Richie Darden," he said softly.

"She lives in a world of white horses and scarlet ribbons. But she's got guts, too. She's a solid woman."

He had his head back again, his face closed, and I couldn't read him.

There was an insistent clamor around Cress and suddenly she lifted her arms, the guitar dangling from one hand, and cried out:

"Reuben—help!"

He stepped into the arena and rescued her.

"She's a strong-minded girl," he said, "and if she won't, she won't. Thanks, Cress, for 'The White Horse Song.'"

He adjusted the guitar to his hand and picked at it idly as Cress made it back to the corner with me. Reuben seemed remote now, abstracted. He paced in a tight circle, his fingers plucking at the strings, searching, as if he didn't know what to do next. Cress moved close and I put my arm around her. Reuben struck some chords and silence fell.

"Little song I picked up," he said, "in my travels. Never sang it before, don't really know how it goes—all the way. Call it—'Man with a Song!'"

He worked on the guitar for some time, his face brooding, and then he began to sing—an odd song, sung by fits and starts, as if he were making it up on the spot.

"Man with a song, a-wanderin'

Singin' a bad song—wanderin';
Plenty of money to fling around,
Scared to death of that mournful sound—
A bad song singin'.
Never go to the Red Dog Tavern.
Stay clear of that high-bindin' breed;—
Take a man's good song
And twist it all wrong
And fill him with pain and greed"

I glanced at Cress and she was still flushed with her own triumph. It seemed to me she was barely listening to Reuben.

Which was just as well, because he was singing straight to me.

"Saw the man with a song go down the road,
Singin' his way down that lonesome road;
Got a lonely, endless way to go
And whether he'll make it I do not know—
A bad song singin'."

He strummed, almost as if in a dead march, deep, heavy chords, then sang the refrain:

"Never go to the Red Dog Tavern;
Stay clear of that high-bindin' breed;
Take a man's good song
And twist it all wrong
And fill him with pain and greed."

The song made a strong impression. Somebody had picked up the refrain and several voices were singing it. Reuben accompanied them for a few bars, then stopped and turned away. I tried to catch his eye, but he avoided me.

That's as much as he'll say, I thought. He knows more, but he can't tell it. It's a code thing. If it hadn't been for Cress he'd never have gone this far.

"That's a pretty good song," Cress said.

"Yeah," I said. "How do you feel? Tired?"

"Yes, a little."

"We'll go when you're ready."

"All right."

Reuben was taking a long break this time and there was quite a lot of milling around. We put Cress's guitar in the case and worked our way to the door, trying in the process to get near Reuben, if only to say good night, but it appeared impossible. Then, as I opened the door for Cress, he caught sight of her and pushed his way through the crowd.

"Thanks for singing," he said. "You let me know where I can reach you and we'll make some arrangement on that song."

"It's all right," Cress said. "You can have it."

"No, that's not a fair way."

"You can reach her through me," I said, "if you want my address."

"Sure."

I got out a card and handed it to him. He looked at it and at me, and there was no expression in his face at all. He put the card in his pocket.

"Thanks again," he said, "and good luck."

"Thanks all around," I said.

"Good night, Reuben," Cress said.

"So long, Cress."

We stepped outside and Cress spread her arms and took a deep breath.

"I sang," she said. "I sang for an audience."

"You sang twice and great," I said.

"I never thought I could do it."

We started down the winding path from the door, among the parked cars jammed in at all angles. There were some lights strung in the trees near the building, but when we got beyond them, it was dark. Cress took my arm and we felt our way toward the street.

"What Reuben was singing," I said, "about the Red Dog Tavern—"

"Gee, I didn't even hear it," she said.

"Is there a real place called the Red Dog Tavern?"

"Yes. In Danville. It's supposed to be a real bad place."

She stumbled and I caught her in time. I had the guitar case in my right hand and we rocked back and forth for a few seconds, getting our balance.

"Dark here," she said.

"Not much farther."

At the street a wooden bridge crossed the deep ditch that separated the road shoulder from the grading cut. A car had pulled well off the road and stood parked in front of mine, which was some twenty feet beyond it. The car had not been there earlier when I had come for the guitar. They had left little space on the shoulder and we had to go single file, squeezing close to the car, to avoid slipping into the ditch. Cress had one hand up against the body of the car to steady herself. She paused once, looking back, then went on and cleared the rear bumper. Then she let out a throaty, thin scream. I saw her spin, start to fall, then right herself, and I saw she had help, the two of them, from behind the car, one hugging her against him with his sleeve covering her mouth, the other with his gun, crowded in close.

I dropped the guitar and got my gun out, but it was useless, with Cress in front of them. I stood there shaking, clawing with my left foot to keep from sliding off the shoulder.

"Don't do it," I said.

"All we want is that suitcase," the one with the gun said. "You get that and bring it here and you can have the girl. Don't yell for any help."

He dropped a piece of white paper to the ground and they started away around the car, backing, holding her in front of them as a shield. I ducked the other way, thinking maybe I could surprise them on the other side, but I saw through the window they had it worked out; they had the back door open and were pushing her into the car, one of them getting in with her, with the gun. I could kill the driver and the one in back could kill Cress, and it was not an even trade. This they could bank on.

The motor roared to life and the car shuddered. I hunched away from it, groping for the guitar. My hand knocked it away and I heard it slide down into the ditch. The car pulled away fast, the tires spitting out gravel, and I ducked my face against it. The piece of paper he had dropped blew into the air and I chased it as if it were a bird, clutching with both hands. I couldn't catch it and had to feel around in the dirt for it as taillights swerved off down the road. I finally found it, noted there was writing on it and crawled down after the guitar. I brought it up, got to the car, threw the guitar in and took off after them. But they had a good start and I knew in my heart where I was going. I was going to the hotel as fast as I could get there and I was going to check out that suitcase and take it exactly where they had written down I should take it, and then we would have to see what would happen after that. The total of what would happen would depend on the condition Cress was in when I got her back.

CHAPTER TWELVE

I didn't take time to go up to the room. I went to the desk, got the suitcase and took it to the car. The message scrawled on the paper was a street and number. I knew nothing of the town and asked a taxi driver, parked in front of the hotel, where the street was. He had to consult a map. It took five minutes for him to plot the route I would take to get there.

"It's way back of town," he said. "What have you got out there?"

"I don't know," I said. "I'll see."

"Well, watch it."

"Where's the Red Dog Tavern?" I asked him.

He looked at me for a few seconds.

"It's in the same neighborhood," he said. "Watch that, too."

"Okay."

It was Saturday night and the streets were crowded. I dragged along the main arteries, not daring to leave the route he had given me. When I finally reached the first turn, the improvement was slight, but after a few blocks the traffic began to thin. The surroundings grew steadily more dingy. I bumped over multiple railroad crossings, past darkened warehouses and elevators. I felt a minute's panic when suddenly there was nothing but open space ahead and I thought I had left the city behind. I could have taken a wrong turn; the taxi driver could have given me a wrong steer out of sheer malice.

Then a new settlement opened up, like a new town, a scraggly twist of streets back of the yards, run-down stores, saloons and stretches of frame houses in bad repair. There were no pedestrians in sight and most of the houses were dark. I had to crawl and turn the nose of the car this way and that to pick up the street names on leaning posts, some nearly illegible. Once I had to leave the car and walk to the post in order to make it out.

I crossed a busy street and by its name I knew I wasn't lost. The driver had told me the truth. A couple of blocks to my right, as I crossed, I read, in garish neon, the name, "Red Dog Tavern."

Beyond the main thoroughfare it was all residential and the pavement gave out. I felt my way over a rutted dirt lane past rows of bleak shacks, some surrounded by picket fences. Once in a while there would be a light in one of them. I traveled three or four blocks—it was impossible to know for certain—and at an eventual corner, nailed to a tree, I saw the name of the street I wanted.

I turned into it and found I couldn't read any house numbers from the car. When there were numbers they were in hiding, up under porch roofs, faded to illegibility on open, sagging gates. I stopped the car, left it, and with the suitcase in one hand and my gun in the other, started walking.

It didn't take long. The number I wanted was the fifth house down the street from where I had left the car. It had no fence, only a weed-choked yard. There was light inside behind tightly drawn shades. The neighboring houses on both sides and most of those across the street seemed uninhabited. There was no sound except for an occasional muted rumble from the railroad yards.

I crossed the few feet from the dirt path that served as sidewalk, mounted a low porch and got to the door. There was no screen door covering it. I used my gun to knock with. Nothing happened and I knocked again. A male voice spoke through the door.

"Who is it?"

"I have a suitcase," I said.

A chain rattled on the other side. The door opened about two inches.

"Just push it inside," the voice said.

It was not the voice of either of the two I wanted.

"What about the girl?" I said.

"Push the suitcase in and I'll hand you the instructions," he said.

Through the crack he left along the edge of the door, across a bare floor, I could see a faded window curtain behind a worn sofa. I set the end of the suitcase against the crack and gave it a push with my foot. He let the door back to admit it. I was holding the gun down along my right thigh and I slid my foot against the bottom of the door as it swung inward.

"The instructions," I said.

A hand appeared between the door and the jamb, a skimpy piece of paper between two of the fingers. I plucked it free with my left hand and he started to close the door. I gave it a half second, to bring him on, then set my shoulder against it and hit the door hard. I heard it bang as he yipped and guessed it had caught him in the head. I kept pushing till I was inside, holding the gun out where it would be plainly visible.

"Hold it," I said.

Halfway across the bare, ill-smelling room, a woman in a kimono was running away toward a door at the rear.

"Stop!" I said.

She kept going. I squeezed off, aiming well to one side of her, and the blast stopped her in her tracks. She seized the doorjamb with both hands and hung on, not looking around.

"Listen…" the man said from my left.

I swung on him with the gun and he backed off toward the center of the room. There was a small table under a floor lamp. Cards were scattered over the table and there were a couple of beer bottles.

"You're making a mistake," he said.

He was a smallish guy in a tight, dark-brown suit, no necktie. There was no sign that anyone besides the two of them were in the house.

"I don't want a piece of paper," I said. "I want the girl, and right away quick now, or somebody will start hurting."

The woman in the kimono started through the door and I barked at her. She stopped. Her head turned slowly and she looked at me across the card table. She was a young woman, but she was sluggish in her movements and her body was sluggish under the kimono.

"Come on back in the room," I said.

She came as far as the table and stood leaning on the back of a chair, holding her kimono over her breasts. The man backed off some more.

"You just stand there," I said.

I glanced at the paper he had handed me and it was blank, both sides, nothing. As I had expected. I wadded it up and threw it away.

"Now talk to me," I said, "and tell me the exact truth. Where do they pick up the suitcase?"

The man brushed at his lapel.

"Go ahead," I said. "If you've got a weapon in there, bring it out. It'll be quicker for you that way."

I stepped toward him and his hands dropped.

"We don't know anything about it," the woman said.

"They'll come here to pick it up?"

Nothing.

"Talk to me," I said.

"Like she said," the man said, "all we know, you were supposed to bring the suitcase."

I walked up to him, grabbed the front of his coat and tore it open. He had a gun in a holster under his arm. He didn't make a move as I took it from him. His face was chalky and he was scared all right, but not enough. I kicked his left knee hard and he fell, with another yip, hanging onto his leg with both hands. The woman started to run again, toward the front door this time. I intercepted and tripped her and she sprawled on the sofa.

"Where are they going to pick up the suitcase?" I asked.

They looked at each other. I started toward the sofa and the woman gathered herself into a tight ball at the end of it. Her eyes watched me with dull resignation and I knew I couldn't get anything out of her without actually hurting her, which I was not prepared to do—yet.

There was a scrambling sound behind me and the man was trying to get out the back way with the suitcase. I started after him, but the woman took care of it for me. She screamed and he stopped.

"You dirty—!" she screamed. "You leave me here alone and I'll kill you, I swear to God I'll kill you…!"

"Come back," I said to him.

He came back and dropped the suitcase between us.

"All right," he said, "take it and beat it."

"Sure," I said, "so I never showed up and maybe they'll believe that. Now listen, this is the last time I ask with my mouth."

I switched the gun I'd taken from him so that I was holding it by the barrel. I hefted it, well out where he could watch.

"Where do they pick up the suitcase?"

He looked at the woman on the sofa and he looked at the suitcase. I lifted the gun in my left hand, as if to start in on him, and he ducked far ahead of time.

"The Red Dog—" he mumbled.

"The Red Dog Tavern?"

"Yeah—"

"All right. Let's go."

"Just him—" the woman said.

"No, both of you. Get dressed."

"I can't—my clothes are in the other room."

"Then we'll all go in there. Come on, shake it up." She got off the sofa and started toward the back of the room. I wiggled the gun in my left hand and the man turned and followed her. I moved in close enough to keep them from thinking anything up, and she switched on a light in a drab, disorderly bedroom. Clothes were thrown across the bed, a skirt, blouse and jacket.

"I'm not interested," I said. "Go ahead and get dressed."

I leaned against the wall, watching the male half—or third, or whatever he was—of the team, while she dressed hurriedly, shedding the kimono only after she had the skirt on, and turning her back to get into the blouse.

"They won't even come in there if they see you," the man said.

"We'll get to that later," I said.

She had her clothes on and was zipping up the jacket.

"You have a car?" I asked.

"No."

"Then we'll walk. I hope you know a short cut."

We went out the front way. The man carried the suitcase and the woman walked beside him. I came along behind, within four strides.

"Go the quickest way," I said, "and don't make a break because I'll use this gun, I promise."

They turned into a narrow alley and I followed them to the next street and into another alley, and so on, block by block. Now and then the woman stumbled and we had to wait for her to get straightened up. But most of the time they moved along all right. It was dark, but there was a glow from the city light and I could see well enough.

I had to figure they would stick to the routine that had been given them. They were between me and them and their choices were limited. If the play had been set up for them to stay in the house with the suitcase, I didn't think they'd dare pull a switch on those two.

And worse yet, I thought, if they get caught trying to make away with it.

We reached the last street but one before the main drag on which the Red Dog fronted. I could see its lights on an acute angle from the street we were crossing, half a block off to the left. One more short length of alley and we reached a paved alley that would run behind the Red Dog and beyond it, bisecting the block. I halted them there.

"We will walk down there, you first," I said, "and not too fast. If your contact is there already, outside somewhere, you will hand over the suitcase and walk away. I advise you to walk fast and not look back. If the contact is not there, we will go inside. I'll give you those instructions when we get there."

They started down the alley. I was close behind them now, using them as a screen, in case the other two should be there, waiting. If they had Cress with them, in the car, they would split up, one to go inside, one to stay with Cress. If they didn't have her with them—we would have to play that one when the music started.

The back entrance to the Red Dog was a metal service door with a heavy wire screen over a frosted window panel. There were trash cans off to one side, and the alley widened to admit delivery traffic and provide a loading zone. Beyond the squat, square building that housed the joint was a parking lot. At a glance it appeared to be full.

"Hold it here," I said.

They stopped. I reached from behind and eased the suitcase out of the man's hand.

"Open one of those trash cans," I said. "Find an empty one."

"What…?"

"Go ahead, do it."

The woman began to whimper. He lifted the lid of one of the cans, replaced it, lifted the next.

"It's empty," he said.

I motioned him clear of it, lifted the suitcase and pushed it down into the can.

"Put the cover on," I said.

He replaced the cover, staring at me.

"All right, let's go in," I said. "You can make a thing of it in there if you have to, but I won't mind tearing the place apart and you with it."

That was empty talk. If they had friends in there and a rough management, I wouldn't have the chance of a feather in a tornado. But so far they had been tractable, and anyway, I had no choice. I couldn't let them go away and I couldn't let them split up and I couldn't stand around in plain sight on the outside.

We went down a wide corridor, past a storeroom and kitchen, and pushed through a heavy swinging door into the tavern. I slid my gun into its holster as we entered. The other was in my pocket and I hoped it didn't show too much.

The place was teeming. There was sawdust on the floor and music thudded out of a jukebox. The interior was L-shaped, with a long bar from the street entrance to the door we had entered, and booths across from it along the wall. Then the room opened out and there was space for dancing, surrounded by booths and some tables. The crowd was a rough one, mainly masculine. There were some couples in the back room, but the bar was men only, in working clothes or suits, according, I guessed, to what was convenient. Half a dozen bartenders were busy serving steins of beer and some hard liquor.

There was one empty table for two in the big room, on the edge of the dance floor.

"You go over there and sit," I said. "Buy a couple of drinks. You have money?"

"Sure," the man said.

"Just go over there and sit and have a drink. And wait for your boy. Don't talk to anyone, just sit and wait and drink. I'll be watching."

They moved uncertainly toward the table. I stood near the swinging door, waiting for someone to get-down from the bar. I saw them take seats at the table and after a while a waitress stop and take their order. I couldn't see that they flashed any signals. I didn't really care much. The tension was in me to the point where I'd have shot it out with the whole place if it should come to that.

A fuzzy-faced old guy in overalls was nodding blearily on the last stool at the bar. The bartenders were all big, beefy guys. One of them leaned across and asked what I wanted. I said I'd wait till I could sit down. He looked at the old man, shook him roughly.

"Hey, Pop," he said. "You had enough."

"Huh?" the old one said.

The bartender gave him a push and I caught him as he fell off the stool. The bartender came around the end of the bar and got his hands under the fellow's arms. He dragged him through the swinging door and was gone about a minute. He came back, got behind the bar and nodded to me.

"Sit down," he said.

I sat down and ordered a beer. By the mirror over the back bar I could see my couple at their table. Some people got up to dance and I found I could keep them in view all right, even when they were momentarily covered by dancing couples.

Toward the front, along the bar, I could watch the front door. The rear entrance was over my left shoulder. I had it covered.

The beer tasted like my own sweat in my mouth and I forced it down, sip by sip.

If they did away with Cress, I kept thinking, I'll have to kill them.

But what if they don't have her and won't talk? I'll have to get help. What kind of help? There isn't any help.

But they won't do away with her before they check on that suitcase. They surely won't. They don't have anything against her, only against me.

Trying to force myself out of the black rut of my mood, I looked around at the place, an ordinary, crummy tavern back of town. The Red Dog Tavern. "Never go...never go..."

Richie Darden was here, I thought. He was in the Red Dog and he ran into those two slugs—when? Months ago. And what for? What was the tangle?

If they don't have Cress—what will I do?

Cut it out now, I thought. You have to go step by step.

The couple at the table ordered another drink. I wondered how they were figuring to crawl out of their foul-up.

That's what was bothering Richie Darden, I thought. He got in a foul-up and had to crawl out of it.

> ...plenty of money to fling around.
> Scared to death of that mournful sound.

Fairmont, I thought. Fairmont, Indiana. Down the road a piece. Something happened a few months back. A payroll robbery.

Richie Darden…?

The swinging door opened over my shoulder and one of them came in, right on my back. Hunched over my beer glass, I saw him by way of the mirror. I was so close, he didn't bother with me. His eyes swept the long bar and switched to survey the booths opposite. My heart was pounding like a storm at the windows.

So they came up the back way, I thought. I get that break.

He looked into the dancing room and my thighs tensed on the stool. I twisted when he spotted the couple at the table. He turned his back on the bar and started in there, and I slid off the stool and shouldered my way past the swinging door.

The service corridor was clear and I hit the rear exit running. All I had going for me was surprise. If the car was out there and Cress in it with the other one, he would move against me first, by reflex, and that would be the break. If the car wasn't there, I'd collar the one behind me and beat it out of him.

The car was there, drawn up across the alley, six long strides from the door. The motor was running and the front door stood open. I saw the other one on the near side of the back seat. He was smoking a cigarette and he had the window rolled down. He saw me coming but had no time to react till I was there. His forearm came over the window sill and there was a gun in his hand. I grabbed his wrist with my left hand and got out my gun with the other. I pulled down hard and his arm straightened and twisted. He made a bad sound in his throat.

"Drop it," I said, "or I'll break it, believe me."

He dropped it. Beyond him a pink bundle lay on the seat.

"Hang on, Cress," I said.

That was all the time I had because the other would be back any second. The one in the car was leaning out the window, trying to get at me with his free hand. I got hold of his coat and pulled him on through, pushing as he fell. He hit the concrete on his head and shoulder and started up groggily. The back door of the joint opened and the other one came out fast. I turned my ankle on the dropped gun and kicked it away under the car.

"Stop!" I said.

He stopped within reach of me. I was shaking and braced myself against the car. The next step was to turn them over. It looked as if I had them now and with some co-operation from the local law could get them in a bottle and up on the shelf. But I had no way to call in the law. I couldn't depend on anybody out of the Red Dog Tavern to be any help, and Cress was lying on the back seat of that car and I didn't know what kind of condition she was in.

"Get going," I said, gesturing with the gun down the alley. "Walk!"

The one I had stopped was in a half crouch, staring at me. The other one had got up and was standing somewhat behind him, looking at the car. Neither of them moved.

"Listen—" the crouching one said.

I hit him across the side of the face with the barrel of the gun and he doubled over, clutching at it with his hands.

"Walk," I said. "That way." I pointed beyond the back of the car. I could feel its vibration against my shoulder blades. "Get started—walk—keep walking…"

I lifted the gun for a moment and the one behind turned and started away, looking back. After a moment the other one got going.

"Faster," I said. "Walk."

I squeezed one off into the ground at their feet and they both jumped and started away at a trot. I ran to the trash cans, jerked the lid off one and lifted out the suitcase. I took it to the car, pushed it onto the front seat and slid in behind it. Far down the alley the two of them had stopped and were looking back. I didn't care anymore. I pulled the door to, put it in gear and drove fast down the alley, a block and a half, turned right onto the dirt road and down to the corner where I had left my car.

I pulled the key from the ignition and threw it as far as I could. It banged against the wall of a house somewhere. I opened the back door and Cress had twisted on the back seat and was staring out at me over a tight gag they had made out of a couple of handkerchiefs. Her hands were tied behind her with some pieces of clothesline. Otherwise she seemed unhurt. I reached in and she fell off the seat onto her knees. I got hold of her and pulled her out and held her with one arm while I got the gag loose and her hands freed. She collapsed against me, gagging and choking. I picked her up and carried her to my own car. When I tried to put her down, her arms tightened around my neck and she clung hard, still fighting to clear her mouth and throat. I walked a little way, carrying her, and walked back.

"You'll be all right now," I said. "All over now."

She said something into my ear, but her words were garbled and I couldn't make it out. I took one arm out from under her to open the car door and she slid down along my body, clinging. I picked her up again and put her in the front seat and closed the door. I ran to the other car, got the suitcase out of it and ran back. When I opened the door on the wheel side, she was clawing at the other door with both hands.

"It's all right, baby," I said. "It's all right now. It's me—Mac."

I pushed the suitcase into the back seat and got in beside her. She came over against me and I held her in one arm while I got it started and turned and headed back the way I had come.

"Did they hurt you?" I said.

"I don't know," she said, and she was crying now. "I don't know. They didn't—do anything—but they tied up my mouth—so tight—"

"All right, it's all over now."

She was shivering violently and sobbing and I held her tightly all the way to the hotel and into the garage. The attendant helped me with her and the suitcase and we took the elevator from the garage to our floor. She was able to walk then, and I could manage the suitcase at the same time and get us into our rooms.

I picked her up and put her on her bed and when I tried to move away, she caught at me.

"They were going to kill me," she said. "They told me—as soon as they got the suitcase—"

"All right," I said. "You're safe now."

I pulled a blanket up from the foot of the bed and covered her, but she went on shivering for a long time. After about an hour I persuaded her to get up and go to the bathroom. While she was gone, I got out of my coat, shoes and took off my tie.

I ought to call the cops, I thought. But they'll be up here right away asking questions, and I can't leave her and I can't have them here with her now.

She came back, walking unsteadily toward the bed. I caught and eased her down and took off her shoes and socks. Then I lay down beside her and covered both of us with the blanket and I held her, sleeping and waking, the whole night long.

CHAPTER THIRTEEN

In the morning she was silent and listless, but no longer terrified, and she let me leave her to bathe and dress. I had not slept much in the night and had done some hard thinking. Among facts I had faced, the crucial one was this: my client was more important to me than the assignment. I was pretty sure I could finish it out, but not with Cress as the stake. The kind of risk we had run the night before was little more than a way of life for me, but this was not true for Cress, and the same would hold for what might lie ahead. The two who, from the start, had deviled us were still on the loose, and now I wanted it that way, for a reason, just a little longer. They surely knew we were at the hotel and surely they would be watching for us to leave it.

As on the morning before, I had breakfast sent up, but she had little appetite. She toyed with her grapefruit, drank her coffee, and her eyes were moody and preoccupied.

"Will you do something for me?" I asked.

"What?"

"Will you go home to your mother and sister?"

"No!"

After a minute her face softened.

"I mean, no, Mac, please don't ask me."

"Just for a visit—"

She shook her head stubbornly.

"I can't go back there."

"They'd be glad to see you—"

"No, they wouldn't."

I must have betrayed disbelief.

"You know what my mother said when I dropped out of school and left home? She said, 'Good riddance.' She hated me, and she hated my father. And my sister was the same."

"Cress, we've run into quite a bit so far—of bad trouble—and we may run into some more."

"All right."

"If you won't go home, will you stay here at the hotel? I'll find some good man to watch out for you and I'll go ahead and trace Richie for you and come back."

She looked around the small room and shuddered.

"Stay here?"

"Just for a couple of days."

Her eyes filled and she shook her head again.

"It's just like in Chicago—at that hotel—I only feel safe with you or Richie. Don't make me stay, Mac."

She got up, came to the back of my chair and put her arms around me and her face against mine.

"Please," she said. "Don't make me stay. I promise I won't panic. I'll do exactly what you say."

"Cress—"

"Besides, I'm ready this time. From now on I'm prepared."

She did a sort of pirouette away from the chair. She was wearing a dress again and nylons and had made a ponytail of her long hair.

"Watch," she said.

She raised her skirt, not coyly, with both hands, and she had a scabbard strapped high on her thigh, with that knife in it, the one I'd told Sergeant Schnell I'd take care of. The picture was so incongruous, I almost laughed but managed not to.

"Where did you learn that?" I asked.

"Richie got it for me. I lied to you," she said. "It's my knife. And he showed me how to wear it—and use it, too."

Her hand made a movement, so quick I couldn't follow it all the way, and came up with the knife, held lightly in the palm of her hand, usable, deadly.

"See?" she said.

"I see."

And I keep trying to argue with her, I thought.

"All right," I said, "we'd better get packed and get out of here, before night falls on us."

We crossed into Indiana shortly after noon and our route led to and followed the Wabash River. It flowed between green banks, rich with willow trees, and the sun glinted from the roofs of the barns and houses of the farms we passed.

"Sing me something," I said.

"Oh—you're just being nice," she said.

"No, I want to hear something. Sing 'The White Horse Song.'"

"I don't know if I can remember it. I gave the words to Reuben."

"You'll remember once you get started."

"Can I get in the back seat?"

"Sure. I'll pull over."

"No, I'll crawl over."

She started over the back of the seat, and with the corner of my eye, as her skirt hiked up, I caught a glimpse of that knife on her thigh. It led me to slow down and study the road behind us. There were several cars, at intervals of three to four hundred yards, and I couldn't see anything of the occupants.

They'll be back there somewhere, though, I thought. I just hope, if she has occasion to use that knife, she'll do it right.

She will, I thought. But if things work out as I expect, she won't have to.

She sang her song, full voice and with confidence. Then, like a good little girl who had done her piece and done it well, she crawled back into the front seat.

"Did you want a horse when you were a little girl?" I asked. "A great white horse?"

"No, I didn't dare think about a big, real horse." After a while she said:

"But once, when I was real little—about four or five—a couple of women took a whole bunch of us to a circus in Danville, thirty or forty kids, I guess. My sister went, too. And at the circus there was this pony ring—you know, some ponies tied on a kind of whirligig kind of rig—and the kids could ride around the ring for a dime. There were so many of us we had to stand in line and wait our turn. And I didn't have a dime left. I'd spent it for something else. But I stood in line—I thought surely something would turn up at the last minute and I'd get to ride a pony anyway. But then my turn came and we were supposed to give our dime to the man and my sister was watching. I didn't have a dime and my sister said I couldn't ride, because I should have saved it. The man said I could go ahead anyway, but my sister wouldn't let me. I cried all the way home and most of that night."

I glanced at her and her eyes were wet. She sniffled and lifted her chin defiantly.

"And that, mister," she said, "if you have to know, is the story of my life at home."

"But Richie Darden changed all that."

"Yes."

Her head moved jerkily and I felt her eyes on me.

"You said something like that once before—kind of snotty—about Richie."

"I didn't mean it to sound that way."

Pretty soon she put her hand on my thigh and her head against my arm.

"Mac, I could love you, if it weren't for Richie. You're the best guy I ever met. But I met him first, you know?"

I hadn't been thinking exactly in those terms, but it was no time to say so.

"I understand," I said.

"Do you know what love is?" Her hand caressed her thigh where the knife was strapped. "Like this knife—in your heart—twisting when anything goes wrong. The night he went away, I thought I'd die. I couldn't sleep. I cried till my throat was so sore I couldn't breathe hardly. I got the knife out. I was going to kill myself, cut my wrists—but I didn't have the nerve."

"You were going to kill yourself?"

"Because—I didn't believe him. I thought he would never come back. I thought he was through with me and gone."

"But later you thought he would come back."

"Yes. Because he never lied to me. Never."

Seventeen, I thought. Everything works by magic.

"Cress," I said, "what do you think is in that suitcase he left with you? What do you honestly think?"

She didn't like the question. Her long little face hardened and her hand left me.

"I don't know," she said flatly. "When Richie tells me, then I'll know."

A road sign's message slapped me gently.

Fallon—6 mi.
Fairmont—15 mi.

"What was the name on that sign?" she asked.

"Fairmont."

"I know, I remember that, but what was the other one?"

"Fallon."

"That's where Sergeant Duffy lived. I remember now. Fallon, Indiana. He had a farm there that his father left him, and that's where he was going when he retired from the army."

"That's good remembering."

"He'll know! Richie would stop to see him. He might even be there now!"

"We'll soon know," I said.

I don't like it now, I thought. It's no good now and it will get worse. What can I say to her?

If only I could sing, I thought.

Gradually I slowed and watched the mailboxes, on posts at the farm roads we passed; the names: Douglas, Moorhead, Acres, Foley, McBride. According to the Fallon paper I had seen, the Duffy farm was two miles west of town, on the riverbank. The road was at some distance from the river and the farms on our right backed up to it. The Duffy place, then, would be on our right, and I didn't bother with the names on the left.

We came to a mailbox I couldn't read. I drifted beyond it, stopped and backed up. The post on which it sat had rotted in the ground and was about to fall over. There had been a name on the box at one time, but it had faded and could not be read from the car. I got out and gave it a close look and it was the one we wanted.

"Duffy," I said, as I got back in the car.

She said nothing but sat forward on the seat, watching tensely as I turned onto the badly kept lane that led to the farm buildings. On both sides the fields had been worked, but there had been no maintenance and evidently little traffic, and weeds grew high along the fences, which were in need of mending.

The sergeant, I thought, hasn't got around to much.

Or maybe, I thought, the sergeant hasn't got home from the army.

The account I had read in the Fallon paper had said only that he was returning to the family homestead. No dates had been mentioned.

Tall trees, elm and oak, surrounded the farmhouse, which was practically bare of paint. The grass under the trees was knee-deep. The lane turned right at the trees and broadened into the yard of the high old barn. Some pieces of rusted equipment filled part of the space. The barn door stood open and there was no tractor in sight and no sign of any living thing—no chickens, pigs, or stock.

I pulled up at the far side of the barn door and turned off the ignition.

"There's nobody here," Cress said.

"It looks as if."

I got out and after a moment she joined me, her small feet cautious in the rank growth of the barnyard.

"We'll go up to the house and make sure," I said.

She held onto my coat sleeve during the walk through the high grass. There had once been a path, but it was overgrown. Sagging steps mounted to a high porch. We climbed up there and I knocked on a solid wooden door. After a while I tried the knob; the door was locked tight.

The porch swept on around one side of the house and there was another door. We tried that one with the same result. There were windows, but shades and curtains were drawn inside and we couldn't see anything of the interior. We went down the side steps and through some more grass toward the rear. There were signs of recent foot traffic here, the grass matted in spots. A few yards beyond a screened rear porch, the land dipped sharply and we were on the high bank overlooking the river. A slope led down, a hundred yards or more, to the willows lining the river course. The path to the river was discernible, a narrow swath in the high grass. It looked in places as if steps had been cut and had gradually weathered away.

"I don't want to go down there," Cress said.

I looked back and her face was drawn tight, frowning.

"All right," I said.

I went down a few strides, feeling the path with my feet. I started to turn back, hesitated and went down a little farther. A metallic wisp had caught my eye, like a thread tangled in the grasstops, a shred of spider's web. But it was more durable than that. I reached for it, curious, and it was a piece of stout wire or string about two feet long. There was a small loop in one end. It gleamed in the sun like steel, but it was lighter than steel. It looked like a musical string, for violin or guitar.

Guitar...

I rolled it up and put it in my pocket. Ahead of me, the path widened abruptly and there was quite a lot of disturbance in the growth, as if some large animal had bedded down there for the night, and not long ago. There were stains, animal-like stains low on the blades, in the grass roots. I pulled some of them up and looked at them. The color was rusty brown, the color a wisp of blood would be after two or three days' drying. I dropped the shreds and dusted my hands.

"Mac—come back, please," Cress called.

She was standing at the top of the slope with both hands extended. I climbed up and put my arm around her.

"I'm afraid here," she said.

"Nothing to be afraid of," I said. "We'll go now, if you want to."

On the way back to the barnyard I took a look down the lane toward the road. There was a bend in it and I couldn't see all the way, but there was no sign of anybody as far as I could see.

They gave up, I thought. I led them too close and they chickened out.

Too bad, I thought. We'll have to try it some other way, or let someone else try it.

At the car I stood looking at the barn for a while. Then I reached into the car and took out my road map and looked at it for a couple of minutes. I tossed the map into the car and walked up to the barn door. After a moment I went inside. Cress hovered in the doorway, her arms huddled across her slender waist.

"What are you looking for?" she said.

"I don't know," I said.

There was a raised deck at one side, bordered by stanchions for cows. At one end was a hay drop. There was a sizable pile of hay on the deck that had been thrown down long before. There was hay in the loft, too, and the roof had leaked and it smelled moldy and corrupt. The pile on the deck was matted down and there was a depression in it, as if something heavy had rested on it.

But that could have been years ago, I thought. It wouldn't spring back necessarily, old dead hay like that.

I kicked at the pile of it with my foot and learned nothing. There were strips of harness hanging on the wall at the end of the deck. On the cross braces between the wall studs were some rusted nuts and bolts, a large crescent wrench, the debris of a dying farm. The studs were about twenty inches apart, and across two of them a couple of old boards had been nailed, as if to form a cubbyhole. There was nothing unusual about that, except that the nails had not been driven home, but protruded a little, and they were shiny, like new nails, or as if the rust had been knocked off them in hammering and hadn't had time to accumulate again.

I reached down into the space between the studs and there were some bundles of paper. I started taking them out. They were bundles of currency wrapped with rubber bands; not old, worn currency, such as a man would hoard in this way, but new currency, crisp and green, and the rubber bands were still tight. I riffled through a bundle and it was made up of ten-and twenty-dollar bills. There were about ten bundles and they were good fat ones.

I gathered them up, carried them to the edge of the deck and tossed them one at a time to the floor. Cress came in slowly, taking short, mincing steps, watching.

"What is that—money?" she said.

"Yes," I said.

"Where did you find it?"

"In here—over there—in the wall."

I sat down on the deck and we both stared at the money for a while.

"Cress," I said, "come here, baby."

She came to me slowly. I put my hands on her waist and held her, feeling her thin, bony knees against mine.

"Cress, I have to tell you something and you won't like it. But it looks like the end of the road and sooner or later—so be a big girl, huh?"

"Go ahead," she said. "Tell me."

"First, let me ask you something. When Richie left the suitcase with you, was it a big secret? I mean, just the fact that he was leaving it with you? Did he tell you not to tell Roger or anyone?"

"No—no secret. He told Roger himself, I remember. When he said goodbye, he told Roger he was leaving some valuables with me."

"In a suitcase?"

"Yes, in a suitcase." She drew back from me, but I held her tightly. "Why?" she said. "Why do you ask me that?"

"I'm just thinking. So there wasn't any secret about the fact that he was leaving the suitcase with you. The only secret was the contents of the suitcase, and that was a secret from you, too."

She didn't say anything.

"The money you gave me," I said, "the hundred dollars. Was that money Richie had left with you?"

"Yes..."

"Let's go get it," I said.

I took her hand and we went to the car and I got out her purse and handed it to her. She looked at me for a moment, then opened it and handed me the thin sheaf of bills. I turned back to the barn and she hesitated, then came after me with quick steps.

I picked up one of the bundles from the floor and started through it, comparing the bills with those Cress had given me. I did it with another bundle, then another. On the fourth bundle I stopped halfway through. I dropped it and Cress's money on top of it and then, because it gave me a feeling of insecurity to see all that money lying on the ground, I gathered it up and stacked it neatly on the deck.

"Listen, Cress—"

I reached for her, but she pulled away suddenly and backed off, deeper into the barn.

"What?" she said. "Go ahead, tell me!"

"About five months ago," I said, "there was a holdup, a big payroll robbery—in Fairmont, Indiana, about ten miles down the road from here. Those two who've been giving us the trouble were part of it—and so was Richie."

"Richie?"

"I don't know how he got talked into it—he was a young guy, carefree, wandering around; maybe it was just another adventure—but it must have started when he ran into those two at the Red Dog Tavern. Reuben practically told us that much."

"Reuben!"

"In the song he sang, the one you didn't hear. What I'm trying to tell you—not like a newspaper account—like a story, the way it must have been. Richie went along with this wild holdup idea and somehow, I don't know how, he came into the loot. And the loot was in the suitcase. And Richie had it and he just kept it and kept going till he got to Chicago, a long way off. And in Chicago he met you and you know about that. But maybe you don't know what was going through Richie's mind all those weeks.

"He had all that money and it didn't belong to him. Doubly. It was stolen to begin with, and then he stole it from his two partners—he may not have meant to; something probably went wrong and there he was with it and he didn't know how to let loose of it.

"Anyway, the worry began to gnaw real hard at him and he began to get scared. He knew from reading the Fairmont papers that the other two were free and he could figure they were looking for him. Maybe he got wind of the fact that they were getting close. Or maybe the pressure just built up to the point where he couldn't sit around and wait any more. He had to go do something; he had to get clear with somebody. But he couldn't turn himself in."

I looked at her and she had her fists balled at her mouth, her eyes staring over them.

"Why should he?" she said. "Would you?"

"I don't know," I said.

"If he had told me—" she said.

"He couldn't. He couldn't tell anybody, and that was about the worst of it. He had only the one person he could turn to—Clare Duffy, the old sergeant. The best friend he ever had. And surely he knew where Clare Duffy's old home was. He would work his way down there, moving back and forth on the way, leaving a winding trail, in case anyone was following him. But even that wasn't enough precaution. And he dreamed up the idea that if he should leave that suitcase with you, and spread the word around, it would stall them off, at least as long as it took them to catch up with you."

"No..." she said.

"And if you put up enough fight, it might stall them for quite a while. So he took off and he worked his way down here. En route he ran into Reuben somewhere, probably others, too. He was in trouble, and some would discern this without being told. Reuben he told, at least part of it. And on top of that, Sergeant Schnell put out a bulletin on him and that's how we ran into that wall of silence about Richie Darden. Everybody wanted to help him."

"Mac—"

"And he got down here and 'Old Sarge' hadn't made it yet. So he just holed up in the barn, to wait."

We looked at each other across the barn floor. She was bent at the waist, holding herself as if she had cramps. Her mouth worked to get the words out. "Then where is he now?"

"I don't know," I said.

"You know everything else—why don't you know that?"

"I don't know."

"I don't believe you. Then what's in the suitcase?"

"Nothing."

"Nothing!" she screamed.

"Nothing at all."

"You're crazy!"

"That may be," I said. "We'll open it and take a look. If there's something in it—anything—I'll take it all back. I'll crawl to Chicago on my hands and knees and you can ride me."

"No—"

"Are you afraid to open it?"

"I promised Richie—"

"Richie left you holding a big fat bag, and you almost died of it."

She was hurting badly and there was nothing I could do to help her, with my voice or my hands or my heart—whatever that is.

What a hell of a way to have to grow up, I thought.

Is it true, I wondered, when she left home, did her mother say "Good riddance"?

I think she did, I thought. I guess she really did.

And now she's got it from the other end—Daddy's no good either. Not even Daddy Richie.

And that was when they showed up.

Three are the things you cannot predict: a woman—and the depth of your own involvement—and the ways of the hunted.

Cress ran out of the barn toward the car. I turned without hurrying, watching her, and saw her swerve, stumble and halt, and stand quivering like an arrow shot into the ground. Then I saw one of them coming from behind the door, a gun in his hand. I was at the barn door by then, with my own gun out. Cress yelled something. The second one was spread-eagled against the barn wall, four feet away, and his bead was drawn between my eyes.

We stood, the four of us, in dead silence for a count of three, and Cress way out in the middle, and I dropped the gun.

"It's in the car," I said. "Go ahead. Take it."

"No," the one by the barn said. "You go get it."

I didn't look at Cress. I just headed for the car. The one behind me moved into line. The other got away from the car, toward Cress.

The suitcase was on the floor of the back seat.

They might just take it and go, I thought, and she'd never know for sure. But it's locked, and where will I get time to work over it?

"Come on with it!" one of them barked.

Lifting it, I twisted the handle so that the case jammed in the doorway. I stepped back and yanked hard, twisting, and saw it spring along the edge where the clasps were, and the lock spread. I yanked once more, and when it came out, it flopped open. I threw it on the ground, the two halves of it exposed, an empty suitcase containing no more than an old splotch of stain, as if a bottle of shaving lotion had leaked in it.

"There it is," I said. "Nothing. And it always was." Naturally they would look into the suitcase, but because there were two of them and Cress in the line of fire, I had planned no heroics. Only one was within reach, at my left, the other six feet away across the open suitcase.

Cress, at home in the jungle of instinct, could not hold back. I cried out inside as her hand pulled at her skirt and the knife flashed in the sun.

The nearer one ducked and swung the gun at her head, but somehow she evaded it. The other started forward. I kicked the suitcase into his legs, and kicking himself free of it, he squeezed off into the air. That gave me a second for the partner, who was lifting his gun hand to slash at Cress. I caught it with both hands and wrenched down and back, pulling him against my legs. The other was leveling off on me and I hit the downed one with his own gun and dived over him.

He fought back, clubbing at me first with his gun, then dropping it because it was useless in the tight give-and-take. He didn't have heart for the fight, but he had desperation and the fury of the ultimately frustrated. He was heavy and hard and I kept hitting him and he kept coming back, falling, getting up again and clawing at me, trying to get hold of me where he could hurt me. I had my own desperation, not knowing what had happened to Cress and the other. All the way to the barn I pushed him and he was still fighting. I slammed him against the wall and when his head bounced I hit him very hard in the jaw and then in the stomach and he quit, gasping, and let himself slide down against the boards, and he sat there.

I wheeled back toward the car, but the other was stretched out on the ground. Cress stood nearby, looking down into the suitcase, still not believing it, and as I came up to her, she threw the knife into the bag and turned away.

I got the keys out of the slot, opened the trunk and found the handcuffs. Why do I keep handcuffs? I thought. Not for this. Why?

I put a set of them on the one who was lying down, prodded him to his feet and pushed him over to the barn. The other one made a tentative feint when I reached for his wrists, but he was through; it was only a gesture.

A shadow fell from the corner of the barn and I ducked. But it was only a man in overalls and a straw hat, looking around, wary, poised to retreat.

"It's all right now," I said. "If you can get to a phone, you might call the sheriff's office. The one in Fairmont."

"Sure thing," he said, and disappeared.

He'd have heard the shooting, I thought.

Cress was walking away from the car, across the barnyard toward the lane that led to the road. I went after her and caught up with her at the corner. She stopped and leaned against a fence post. When I touched her, she jerked away from me.

"We'll have to wait till the police come," I said. "Then we'll go."

"Where?" she said. "Where will we go?"

"Home," I said.

I looked back toward the barn, and one of them had got on his feet and started away, his hands locked in front of him. The other stuck out one foot and tripped him. I went over there and pulled him back against the wall.

I went into the barn and picked up the bundles of currency. I carried them to the suitcase, dumped them in there and took the suitcase back to where they were sitting. When I dropped it, to let them see, they just looked at it with blank faces.

Cress was far off, leaning against the fence. I started over there, stopped and looked back, and then I stood in the sun, waiting.

CHAPTER FOURTEEN

There was only one officer, in a car bearing the sheriff's insignia in gold on a black door. He was what the newspapers would describe as a grizzled veteran of the service. He was stocky and gray, with narrowed lids over blue eyes. There was a scar on his left cheekbone where somebody had hit him at one time and the wound had been badly stitched. He had pulled up in the car near where I stood and he took his time getting out, his face a quiet question. I pointed to the barn.

"Something over there you may want," I said.

He gave me a look and we went over to the wall, where he stooped and looked at them for a moment.

"Sure do," he said. "I sure do."

I helped get them into the back seat of his wagon. He had the wire screen across the seat and no handles on the doors and I guessed he would be able to handle it all right. I was not going to insult him by offering to assist him on the ride home.

He examined the currency in the suitcase at some length.

"Is it from that payroll job?" I asked him.

"It looks as if it is," he said. "Yes, sir, it looks like it. Don't know if it's all here."

"I don't think it is, but quite a lot."

"Yup. Quite a lot."

He carried the suitcase and the loot to the car and put it in the front seat. He got out a pencil and notebook and said:

"Who are you?"

I told him I was from Chicago. He looked toward the lane, where Cress leaned against the fence.

"Who is the young lady?"

"A friend," I said. "We were just hoping to talk to Sergeant Duffy."

"Oh. Well, the sergeant won't be here, I understand, for a couple of weeks. You know how it is getting out of the army—"

"Sure."

"And you were just hanging around here and all of a sudden she popped—them two?"

"In a way."

He squinted and his mouth twitched. I wasn't giving him very good answers. But then his questions weren't too probing.

"The money was hidden in the barn, between a couple of studs," I said. "You can see where the fresh nails are."

He jerked his head slightly and passed his hand over his eyes, as if distressed. I started over toward the fence where Cress was and he came along with me. He deserved more explanation than I had given him. I took out my wallet and showed him my license.

"Oh," he said. "How'd you get onto the payroll robbery?"

"I just happened to read about it. We don't have anything to do with it. We just got kind of slapped with it."

Cress looked at us from the fence, her face hooded.

"Tell us about the payroll job," I said. "What happened?"

He looked back toward his car.

"Well," he said, "it's kind of a long story—"

"Not much to ask, is it," I said, "for what we just handed you?"

"Come to think of it," he said, "there's a reward—"

"Not interested," I said. "But what happened?"

"Well, I was there," he said. "We got this house-wares plant in Fairmont, big plant, you'd know the stuff they make. Payroll runs about sixty, seventy thousand a week. The regular routine was one of the trucks, you know, would run the cash out there, from the bank in town, on Friday morning. But this particular week, they come up against a bank holiday and some other stuff and the paymaster planned to take a guy along with him and pick it up in his car on Thursday, along toward evenin'. So they called me to see if I would ride along and I would.

"The plant road is outside of town quite a ways and it's bushy around there. Also it was the bad time of day, bad light. Not that I want to make excuses, but that's the way it was.

"Well, sir, I don't know how in the world these whelps got wind of the change in the schedule—somebody inside must have tipped them, but we never did find out who. Anyway, we turned into the road and they were waitin' for us. We saw a car comin' when we turned in, but it stopped to give us the right of way and we didn't think anything of it. Then we made the turn and two of 'em—them two—were in the bushes and come up with guns, one on each side of the car. The third one was in that other car, waitin', right at the turn.

"Can't explain it except that everything went wrong the way it sometimes does. They had a gun at the paymaster's head—he was drivin'—and I couldn't make a move. I told him to do like they said, and he handed over the bag he had the cash in, and then one of 'em come up with a suitcase from behind a bush and opened it and stuffed the bag in the suitcase. All the time the third one is sittin' there in the car, waitin', and the one with the gun, on the paymaster's side, motioned us to go ahead. I thought then I could see a way to handle it, so when the car started up, I opened my door and got out, keepin' down low, and I braced both of 'em just as they were pickin' up the bag.

"Don't know why they didn't just shoot me, but for some reason, instead of that, one of 'em swung on me with his gun. It caught me pretty good and I stumbled and I was blazin' by then anyway, so I just piled into 'em with both hands. And while we were at it, the one in the car, he must have jumped up and grabbed the suitcase and beat it. I heard the car goin' away while we were still mixin' it up."

He paused, squinted, spat on the ground and looked defensive.

"I wasn't a match for the two of 'em," he said. "They beat me right down to the ground, and when I come to, they were gone and so was the suitcase. And that was the last I see anything of 'em, or anybody else for that matter, for five months—until today. But I got a good memory for faces, and it's them all right."

I glanced at Cress. She was standing stiffly against the post with her hands at her sides, and I couldn't tell whether she was listening or not.

"I got a good look at the one in the car, too," he said. "Believe me, I did. And we got him. Yes, sir."

"You got him?"

"Just the other day," he said. "Right here. Don't know why he come back, never had a chance to ask him."

"How did you—get him?" I asked.

"Well, Jed White, got the farm next door, called up and said there was a young fellow hanging around the Duffy barn. Said he looked to be sleepin' there. Couple of days. So I drove out and sure enough, there he was, sittin' on the fence in the sun, eatin' an apple. And I spotted him right away, but I guess he couldn't see how I would have known him. He didn't make any move. He sat there and said he was just travelin' through the country and he stopped for the night and slept in the barn and he was sorry if it was against the law, he'd move on, and like that.

"He took me in the barn and showed me. He had this guitar with him, in a case, and a little satchel, and he said he was travelin', pickin' up songs. So then I mentioned the payroll holdup. He got scared right away. 'You were drivin' the car,' I told him, 'and you grabbed the suitcase and run for it. So just come along with me.'

"And then he made his mistake. He swung the guitar case at me and he took off. He run out of the barn and around there toward the back of the house, and I went after him, yellin' at him to stop and gettin' my gun out, because what else could I do? And he got to the bank there, behind the house, and started down toward the river, in the grass, and the guitar case flyin' beside him, and from the bank I yelled at him to stop and he kept on goin' and I shot him. I'm a pretty good shot and when I let go, if he would have been goin' in a straight line, I would have hit him in the leg, or the behind. But he was runnin' and twistin' and it hit him in the back and it killed him."

He looked away toward the house and beyond it over the river.

"Right over there, just the other day," he said. "I'm sorry it turned out that way. But what else could I do?"

I tried to look at Cress, but I couldn't.

"Yeah," I said. "Well, you better get on to town with your load." I got out a card and handed it to him. "You can get hold of me if you want any more details on what happened today. I'll come back and testify if necessary."

"All right," he said. "And I appreciate what you did."

"Don't mention it," I said.

He walked away and got in the car and drove off without wasting any time. I think he was nervous about being alone with the two of them and wanted to get it over with. I couldn't blame him.

Finally I looked at Cress. She was half turned against the post, her fingers clutching at the top strand of the fence, as if to hold herself up.

"Where?" she said, her voice thin, stringy. "Where did he die?"

"Cress—let's go now."

"I want to see where."

She pushed away from the post. I caught her arm and she let me guide her to the rear of the house and the high grassy bank. She looked down that shimmering swath where the grasstops swayed apart, down the way Richie had taken.

"Down there?" she said.

"Yes, Cress."

"You went down there—before. Did you see? Did you know he died there?"

"I'm not sure," I said. "I think I did. But I'm not sure."

I took the guitar string out of my pocket and tossed it down. It gleamed for a moment, twisting in the sunlight, and came to rest in the grass, like a spider web, a wisp of silver thread.

Cress turned away and I followed her to the car, not touching her, but close enough to help her if she should stumble.

"Where do you want to go?" I asked.

"Back to Chicago," she said.

I helped her into the car and we got started.

* * * *

I drove quite fast, but it was dark when we crossed the state line. To avoid dragging through Danville, I took the alternate route to the south, through the college town where we had heard Reuben. I wasn't thinking about Reuben at the time, but I had it in the back of my head that maybe she would change her mind—maybe she would want to go to her own home town—maybe it was different inside her now.

But I had no way to read what was in her mind. She sat on the far side of the seat, jammed against the door, her eyes wide open and blank, empty as the windows of a deserted house.

We were approaching the town, with the campus ahead on our right, on the hills, when she put both hands on her stomach, pressing.

"I need something," she said. "Coffee."

"We'll find a place—"

"There's a place here," she said.

I had to brake sharply to make the turn into the little coffeehouse. There were parking spaces tonight and I pulled up near the door. We got out and she opened the back door and got her guitar.

There were fifteen or twenty kids in the place, scattered around the room, some sitting by the fire. There was music coming from a hi-fi in a corner of the room. Nobody took any special notice of us as we entered, and a girl took our order for coffee and brought it—without whipped cream—and we sat over it.

After a while the waitress came to the table, somewhat shyly, and said:

"You were here last night?"

"Yes," I said.

"You're the girl who sang 'The White Horse Song.'"

Cress looked at her and nodded. The waitress went away, and I guess she started spreading the word. In about five minutes they were asking Cress to sing.

My God! I thought. What is she like inside? Why did she want to stop here?

She didn't acknowledge any of the clamor, but pretty soon she took out her guitar and, seated, tuned it and plucked at the strings. After a while she got up and walked to the center of the room and settled something in the strings. She began to sing, low and whispering at first, familiarly, her tone gradually rounding.

It was that love song she had sung the first night I'd met her, in the hotel, when she cried.

> *"The joys of love*
> *Are but a moment long;*
> *The pain of love endures*
> *The whole life long."*

Her voice strengthened as she sang. She wasn't crying this time. She sang it through to the end, but not really ending; something in the strings was unfinished, unresolved. Her fingers seemed to fumble among the chords. Then they found what they wanted. Her voice rose again, very clear and high, a different tone, such as I had never heard in her voice before. It rang in the room like the cry of a bird in pain.

> *"And his name was Richie Darden—*
> *And his sweet voice I can never forget."*

Suddenly I was staring down at my coffee cup. I started to pick it up, then put it down again, not daring to lift it to my mouth. My vision had fogged and I would have to wait until it cleared.

Cress, I thought. Crescentia…Crescentia Fanio.

Singer.

www.ingramcontent.com/pod-product-compliance
Lightning Source LLC
Chambersburg PA
CBHW020658180626
46816CB00003B/1336